OPEN MIC

OPEN MIC

Riffs on Life Between Cultures in Ten Voices

edited by

Mitali Perkins

CANDLEWICK PRESS

Compilation and introduction copyright © 2013 by Mitali Perkins
"Becoming Henry Lee" copyright © 2013 by David Yoo
"Why I Won't Be Watching the *Last Airbender* Movie"
copyright © 2010 by Gene Luen Yang
"Talent Show" copyright © 2013 by Cherry Cheva
"Voilà!" copyright © 2013 by Debbie Rigaud
"Three-Pointer" copyright © 2013 by Mitali Perkins
"Like Me" copyright © 2013 by Varian Johnson
"Confessions of a Black Geek"
copyright © 2013 by Olugbemisola Rhuday-Perkovich
"Under Berlin" copyright © 2013 by G. Neri
"Brotherly Love" copyright © 2013 by Francisco X. Stork
"Lexicon" copyright © 2013 by Naomi Shihab Nye

The traditional verse on page 114 is from *Poems for the Children's Hour,*
compiled by Josephine Bouton (New York: Platt & Munk, 1945).

First paperback edition 2016

Library of Congress Catalog Card Number 2012955218
ISBN 978-0-7636-5866-3 (hardcover)
ISBN 978-0-7636-9095-3 (paperback)

18 19 20 21 BVG 10 9 8 7 6 5 4 3 2

Printed in Berryville, VA, U.S.A.

This book was typeset in Stone Print and Stone Sans.

Candlewick Press
99 Dover Street
Somerville, Massachusetts 02144

visit us at www.candlewick.com

To my nephews, Jason and Jordan,
who know about life between cultures

CONTENTS

INTRODUCTION

Conversations about race can be so *serious,* right? People get all tense or touchy. The best way to ease the situation is with humor. There's actually a lot of bizarre comedy material when it comes to growing up "between cultures," as I like to call it. It's a weird place.

Take being Indian-American, for example. Why did that lady at the grocery store feel compelled to tell me about her random bad experience with chicken tikka masala? Do I want to know? We don't even eat chicken tikka masala in my part of India. It's just as orange and soupy and strange to me as it is to her.

And did that dude *really* just ask if I know his doctor? There are over a billion of us on the planet—why should

Dr. So-and-So-ji and I be best buddies? (It's even stranger when I *do* know his Indian doctor, which happened once.)

Then there's the boring dinner party conversation during which an artsy type describes—in lengthy detail, ad nauseum—the plot of that one Bollywood movie he simply *adored*. I grew up with those "fillums," man. There are a bunch of them. It only makes things worse when you apply a weird lilting accent, add a head waggle, and laugh hilariously at yourself. Awkward.

What works better (at least for me) is when *I* share stories about how strange it was to be squeezed between cultures. Like when I was seven and wondered why the fat guy in the red suit skipped our house completely in December. And then some stupid bunny forgot to come in April. Or later, in high school, wanting desperately to date guys, which wasn't going to happen because (a) I was the color of pastrami and they preferred provolone, and (b) my parents dated *after* they met and got married, both of which happened on the same day.

When I tell my stories, I want listeners to laugh (not *at* me, I hope, but *with* me). Humor has the power to break down barriers and draw us together across borders. Once you've shared a laugh with someone, it's almost impossible to see them as "other." Poking fun at my marginalized life also sets readers free to see the funny in their own lives, a key to surviving the stressful experience of becoming an adult.

I do have some ground rules, however, for what I consider good humor, especially in a tension-filled arena like race. Here they are, take them or leave them:

1. *Good humor pokes fun at the powerful—not the weak.* Using the gift of wit to pummel someone less gifted physically, socially, emotionally, or intellectually may win a few initial laughs. Soon, though, audiences sense the power-flexing of a bully behind the humor, and they'll stop listening. The most powerful person of all, of course, is the storyteller (see rule #3), so no holds barred when it comes to humbling that target.

2. *Good humor builds affection for the "other."* At the close of a story, poem, or joke about race or ethnicity, do we feel closer to people who are the subject of the humor? If not, even if the piece is hilarious, it's not *good* funny. Sometimes comedians use wit to alienate the "other" from us instead of drawing us closer to one another. Again, they may get a few laughs, but they're cheap laughs. Of course, I don't like *any* humor where someone gets hurt—I rooted for Wile E. Coyote, winced at the Marx brothers' physical (painful) humor, and stand stony-faced while my sons laugh at videos of people falling and crashing into things. So take rule #2 with a caveat: if watching someone take a hit or a blow makes you like them better, you might appreciate some humor that I don't. And that's okay.

3. *Good humor is usually self-deprecatory* (note: not self-defecatory, although it can feel like that). While I usually don't like edicts about who can write about whom, in a post-9/11 North America, where segregation, slavery, and even genocide aren't too far back in history, funny multicultural stories work best when the author shares the protagonist's race or culture. Funny is powerful, and that's why in this case it does matter who tells a story. Writing that explores issues of race and ethnicity with a touch of humor must stay closer to memoir than other kinds of fiction on the spectrum of storytelling. Some writers and comedians have succeeded in poking fun across borders, but it's challenging in today's mine-filled conversations about race. Go ahead if you want to try, I tell them, but don't say I didn't warn you.

Okay, enough with the rules. Time for some lighthearted storytelling about the between-cultures life. I'm thrilled about the authors who have contributed to this anthology. Some pieces, like Cherry Cheva's "Talent Show," Debbie Rigaud's *"Voilà!"* and David Yoo's "Becoming Henry Lee," make us chuckle; others, like Greg Neri's "Under Berlin," Francisco Stork's "Brotherly Love," my "Three-Pointer," and Varian Johnson's "Like Me," may bring a rueful, ouch-filled smile. Gene Luen Yang's "Why I Won't Be Watching the *Last Airbender* Movie," Olugbemisola Rhuday-Perkovich's "Confessions of a Black Geek," and Naomi Shihab Nye's "Lexicon" make us feel like we're exchanging a knowing glance of shared humor with the storyteller or poet—like viewers are supposed to feel when cast members on popular sitcoms catch the camera's eye for a moment.

When you're done reading, or if something strikes your fancy, find us on Facebook (facebook.com/openmicanthology) to let us know what you think, and share your own weird, funny, or crazy story about growing up between cultures.

Laughing with you, not at you,
Mitali Perkins

Becoming Henry Lee

DAVID YOO

Ching Chong's real name was Henry Choi Lee, but when he started the eighth grade, one of his classmates called him Ching Chong and it stuck. At first this bothered him — who wants to be called Ching Chong, after all? — but it would soon turn out that what his classmates called him was the least of his problems.

Before his father was transferred to Connecticut for his job, the Lees lived in southern California, where Henry was surrounded by other Asian students. But at Renham Middle School in Renham, Connecticut, he was the only Asian kid.

Renham was an affluent town and home to the best high school in Connecticut, which was the main reason Henry's parents had moved there. They wanted to give their son a leg up toward getting into an Ivy League university, which would then give him the best chance of eventually becoming a doctor or lawyer. "A doctor or lawyer command respect in community," they'd often say.

"So does proper grammar," Henry would retort, but they'd ignore him.

The adult Lees fit some of the Asian stereotypes nicely. But not Henry. Everyone at school assumed he was a nerd. They were certain he was a whiz at numbers, music, video games, and kung fu. Like all Asians must be.

But in fact, Henry was horrible at math and could hardly play the piano despite the private lessons his parents had arranged for him since he was four. He got dizzy playing first-person shooter games because of a balance problem caused by the perpetual inflammation of his inner ear. Which also meant that when it came to martial arts, Henry was clueless.

Within a month of starting eighth grade in this new town, Henry decided that he absolutely hated being Korean. Or rather, he didn't like being different. He made it his main goal to change people's perceptions of him. So he never studied and swore off video games (which he didn't like playing anyway) and Asian food.

At the Renham Galleria food court, Henry made it a point to eat pizza (even though the slices were always a little cold) and avoided the comic-book store and gaming depot. The cool white boys in his grade sat with their equally cool girlfriends, whose dyed hair always came out kind of blue-looking instead of the intended black, and ate the teriyaki combo #3 from Chang Gourmet after spending hours reading manga and trading used video games.

Another problem, at least as Henry saw it, was that people could tell from a mile away that he was Asian. So Henry started wearing white baseball caps with the brim pushed down low, trying to hide his jet-black hair and smaller, upper-eyelid-deprived Asian eyes. One weekend, after watching an episode of some Nickelodeon show where the star had bright blond hair and was beloved by everyone, he ran out to the store, bought a bottle of Color-Me-Blond, and dyed his hair. At school on Monday, he hated himself for not thinking through his decision. Kids kept asking him if "the carpet matched the drapes," which Henry didn't quite understand, given that they'd never before seemed interested enough to inquire about his house, though deep down he had a feeling it had something to do with the fact that his newly blond hair clashed with his still-black eyebrows.

Kids also teased Henry by pretending to talk in broken English, even though he had a perfectly good American accent. He decided he had to make it even more obvious that he didn't speak the way they thought a Korean would. The following weekend, he decided to adopt a southern accent, so he rummaged through his parents' old DVD collection. Unfortunately for Henry, the one movie the Lees owned that took place in the South was their boxed set of *Roots,* an epic

TV miniseries about slavery. That Monday students were more confused than convinced by his new accent.

"Late for class again, Ching Chong?" a kid asked as Henry struggled to open his lock.

"Never you mind, boy," Henry replied in his best *Roots* voice. "I hear tell the teacher's fixing to be late for class on account of the coffee machine in the lounge being done busted, so he gone have to get his coffee from down yonder in the cafeteria where done —"

"Chinese sure sounds a lot like English," the kid said. "What the heck did you just say?"

Dashing off to class, Henry tried to get a laugh by insulting the teacher in his new voice. "Lawd almighty, I done hear tell you smells right like a hawse," he told her. Sadly, his classmates didn't understand what the heck he was saying. The teacher must have, though, because she gave him three days of detention.

For the rest of the day, Henry simplified his southern accent by sticking the word *ain't* into every other sentence. Nobody paid much attention. Obviously, his linguistic efforts were failing to convince anyone that he was a white boy whose daddy owned a plantation.

When Henry's mom picked him up after school, Henry was so depressed that he didn't see her pull up. She rolled down the driver's side window and hollered, "Henry! You get in car, now!"

"Yeah, Ching Chong, you get in car, now!" the other kids hooted.

Henry hurried to the car, embarrassed by his mom's broken English. The next afternoon, even though he lived several miles away, Henry walked home after detention. His mom saw him walking down West Renham Road and slammed on the brakes.

"What are you doing? Traffic is dangerous! Get in car now!" she shouted.

"Thought I'd save you some gas," Henry said, looking around feverishly before diving into the backseat.

Thanks to the unchangeable shape of his eyes and his parents' undeniable Asian accents, Henry realized he was never going to convince his peers that he was white. It was going to take a miracle for things to turn around, but luckily for Henry, a miracle was waiting for him in study hall the first day back from winter break: Marcy Spetucchi, the most popular girl in the eighth grade. And although she had never said a word to Henry before, when Marcy saw Henry sitting there all alone, she asked him out of the blue, "You're good at math, Ching Chong. Can you help me with my homework?"

Up to this moment, Henry had always gotten frustrated when classmates asked him for help on math homework, but this time, he agreed. Marcy was too pretty to deny. As he taught her how to do math, making up rules and formulas as he went along, he realized that he'd finally stumbled upon the solution to his social woes. He'd been going about it all wrong, it turned out; rather than trying to convince everyone he wasn't Asian, the key was to become über-Asian. Wasn't this proof? For the first time ever, Henry Choi Lee was hanging out with the most popular girl in school.

After school that day, he accompanied his one sort-of friend (a pale, perpetually bloody-nosed kid named Sam, who lived down the street) to the mall, where they happened upon a group of kids from a rival middle school talking smack with kids from Renham.

Henry decided to test his new theory. He stalked over to the fight, crouched low, and started growling and shoving air around with his hands.

At first his classmates looked as stunned by his maneuver as their rivals, but then one of them moved closer to Henry. "You mess with us, you mess with the Karate Kid," he said.

"Yeah, Henry could kick anyone's butt at Farnham," another one added. "He's got a fourth-degree black belt in kung fu."

"For real?" one of the Farnham middle-schoolers asked.

Henry nodded and kept yowling. For the first time, he saw his classmates beam at him.

"Why's your nose bleeding?" the rival kid asked Sam.

"He got out of line," Henry muttered ominously.

The Farnham kids backed off, and his classmates gleefully patted him on the back. As Henry fist-bumped them one by one, he wondered why he'd hated stereotypes so much. What was so wrong with people mistakenly assuming he was a genius? That he was good at math and science? That he was a martial arts master? Obviously the key was to prove that he was the most *Asian* Asian student in the history of middle school.

That weekend he did research online on how to be Asian and began crafting a persona that incorporated all the major elements of Asian-ness imaginable. His first move was to use tai chi and meditation.

In gym class, Mark Porter shouted in pain as his back seized up from trying to do a pull-up. As he writhed around like a grub on the cushioned mat while the rest of the class and the gym teacher stared at him in fascination, Henry gravely walked to Mark and stood over him. He clapped his hands loudly once to get everyone's attention, then proceeded to rub them really fast like he was trying to warm them up. Mark looked up at Henry, puzzled but still making appropriate sounds of pain.

"I will now use tai chi to help your back feel better," Henry said, and closing his eyes, he proceeded to move his arms in a dance-like motion à la Mr. Miyagi, pretending to shoot waves of *chi* into Mark's back.

A moment later, Mark stopped groaning. "I think I feel something," he said, keeping his eyes on Henry.

"Usually you do tai chi on yourself, to relieve stress,"

Henry explained, "but if you're really one with the life force, it's okay to use it on others. What I'm doing here is redirecting positive energy to your back while at the same time pulling away the . . . er . . . evil energy." Henry shook his head slightly as he concentrated with his eyes closed.

"It's working!" Mark said.

Henry opened his eyes. Everyone, even the gym teacher, was looking at him like he was some kind of Zen wizard.

By the next morning, circles were forming around Henry wherever he went. Students wanted to see him perform tai chi again, but they were hesitant. Finally, a kid asked if Henry could help his strained wrist feel better.

"I only have a certain amount of *chi* to work with each week. Maybe next week," Henry said.

"But—" the student protested.

"I said be ready for you next week!" Henry shouted, imitating the angry Chinese dry cleaner who yelled that exact same grammatically incorrect sentence at his dad any time Mr. Lee tried to pick up his dress shirts.

Some of the students didn't believe in Henry's magical tai chi abilities, so in homeroom, he decided to prove them wrong. Extending a stiff index finger, he zapped one of the beta fish in the bowl on Mr. Parson's desk with a dollop of invisible *chi*. Nothing happened.

"The fish is fine," a skeptic noted.

"Not so, young grasshopper," Henry said, lightly patting

the kid on the back. "I just used *chi* to scramble its internal organs. You'll see: in a few days that fish will be dead."

Sure enough, a few mornings later, the students arrived to find one of the beta fish lying sideways at the top of the water. Everyone was officially convinced that Henry was a tai chi master. No one seemed to remember that before Henry's zap, beta fish seemed to die every few days since they didn't have long life spans to begin with.

The kid with the wrist injury approached him again for his services.

"It seems pretty serious," Henry said, feeling the kid's wrist. "We might need to do some acupuncture. I don't have my needles with me. Why don't you go sharpen a half-dozen pencils, and we'll see what we can do about this wrist pain you speak of."

The kid raced off without a moment's hesitation, and Henry was taken aback. Wasn't the threat of getting punctured by pencils enough to deter this patient? The kid returned, clutching a handful of newly sharpened pencils. "Um, wait—are those lead pencils?" Henry stalled. "Yeah, no, that's not going to work. Let's just stick with the tai chi."

Pretending to know stuff was exhausting. Henry almost fell asleep in English class. The teacher shouted for him to wake up, and Henry, startled at first, glanced at his peers before explaining, "I wasn't sleeping. I was meditating."

The teacher rolled her eyes, and Henry leaned over to

James Murphy to whisper, "I used my meditation to visualize tomorrow's multiple-choice quiz. Choose *B* when you don't know the answer."

This, of course, hadn't come from meditating. The "*B* strategy" was something he'd learned about multiple-choice questions when his parents had forced him to take a PSAT training course the summer before.

The best part about amping up his Asian-ness was that he got to spend time with Marcy Spetucchi. Because he was bad at math, Marcy didn't learn how to do the problems correctly. When she failed her next quiz, Henry shrugged and said, "I guess you're going to have to work harder at it." She begged Henry to be her full-time math tutor every day after school. "You're not like the other boys," she said, smiling shyly at him.

Two more failed quizzes later, and Marcy finally realized the real reason he was different from the other boys: he was really, really bad at math, and something of a compulsive liar. She promptly fired him. Or dumped him. Depending on whom you asked. However, others had noticed them spending time together, and by the end of the year, people seemed to see Henry in a new light. In fact, nobody called him Ching Chong anymore!

Summer came and went with more SAT prep. When Henry got to Renham High, he was ready to take his role of Super Asian Man to the next level. Unfortunately, he ran into a problem. There was one other Asian student in the high school, Timmy Nguyen, valedictorian of the senior class, which changed everything. The whole student body now regularly mistook Henry (mistakenly or intentionally—what difference did it make?) for this Nguyen fellow, even though the senior was Vietnamese and looked nothing like Henry (the guy even had a full mustache and Henry hadn't started shaving). Upper-class nerds shoved Henry into the lockers, assuming that (a) he was Timmy, or (b) he was a curve buster just like Timmy, even though Henry was bombing his classes and hurtling toward a decidedly un-Asian low GPA. His own former classmates from middle school ignored him again, since being unquestionably Asian was not considered cool at Renham High.

One weekend Henry's parents rented the movie *The Departed*, in which two white actors—Leonardo DiCaprio and Matt Damon—played foes. As they watched the crime drama together, Henry was stunned to discover that his parents had mistaken the two actors for the same person. They were convinced the movie was a psychological thriller about one white guy who had multiple personalities warring with each other in his head.

"Hold on," his dad said, pointing at the screen for the dozenth time. "Is he the good cop now or the bad cop?"

Suddenly Henry was beyond mad—his white classmates thought all Asian guys looked the same, and his parents thought all white guys looked the same, too? Was he the only person on the planet who noticed that people of the same race weren't all twins or clones? "You guys are racist!" Henry shouted, and ran upstairs to his room.

His father eventually followed him upstairs and sat next to Henry on the edge of his bed. It was equally uncomfortable for them both. When his father asked what was wrong, Henry explained everything: from when he'd first started school in Renham to now, when everyone was mistaking him for Timmy Nguyen.

Mr. Lee thought about this for a minute before responding. "Well, things could be worse," he said. "For instance, take this Timmy Nguyen person. Imagine the poor guy, being mistaken for *you*."

This failed to cheer Henry up, so his father thought about it some more.

"Maybe if you give classmates something to identify you, they don't think you're someone else," he said. "Besides, you need do more extracurricular activities so you stand out to admissions committees at Ivies."

Clearly his father was still trying to get Henry to become the cliché Asian son he'd always wanted, but Henry decided to take his advice anyway. The next morning, when his homeroom teacher asked for a volunteer to help a classmate read a scene for drama-club auditions, Henry raised his hand. After hearing Henry's line reading, the classmate encouraged him to try out for the play.

At the audition, everyone was stunned at how good an actor Henry was.

"Do you have any experience?" the drama teacher asked.

"Not really," Henry said, but he realized this wasn't entirely true, because ever since moving to Renham, he'd been acting—wasn't the definition of acting pretending to be somebody you weren't?

"You're a natural," the drama teacher said.

And so just like that, Henry finally found himself a full-fledged member of a group. After tryouts, they headed for the late buses, where they ran into the JV wrestling team, who shouted, "Drama queens!" and "Fairy losers!"

The actors were furious and shot back insults, but not Henry. He smiled blissfully, repeating the taunts in his head as if they were the most beautiful sounds he'd ever heard.

Drama queens . . . Fairy losers . . .

The plural was music to his ears.

Why I Won't Be Watching the Last Airbender Movie

GENE LUEN YANG

Derek was the first to tell me about it.

I knew they would do something like this! *I knew it!*

Award-winning cartoonist Derek Kirk Kim

It's an Asian fetishist's *dream!* All the Asian culture you could want without any of those pesky Asian people!

We've gotta respond in some way!

And so we did.

Derek wrote a blog post explaining our anger and advocating for a boycott.

I drew a webcomic doing the same. I posted it on my website a month before the movie's release.

WHY I WON'T BE WATCHING THE LAST AIRBENDER MOVIE

A friend turned me on to the original *Avatar: The Last Airbender* animated series on Nickelodeon, and from the first episode, I was hooked!

Gene Luen Yang, author of *American Born Chinese*

Here was an American cartoon with multi-faceted characters and addictive plot lines, all set in a beautifully constructed Asian fantasy world.

The writing was not only witty, thoughtful, and clever; it also showed a deep respect for and knowledge of Asian cultures. Even my wife loved it, and she usually avoids cartoons like the plague.

Don't you see?! The politics of the Fire Nation reflect those of Japan during the Meiji Restoration!

Shut up. They're gonna fight again.

When I heard that they were going to make a live-action adaptation, I was *thrilled*—

Oh, my flying Appas! That's gonna be amazing!

—until I learned they'd given the roles of the major heroic characters—all of whom were Asian or Inuit in the cartoon—to white actors.

What?!

Look, don't you want to live in a color-blind society? Maybe the most qualified actors for those roles just happened to be white!

Maybe...

Airbender's advocate

... but then how do you explain the original casting calls, which clearly indicated a preference for white actors from the get-go?

12-15 years old, Male, **Caucasian or any other ethnicity.** We are looking for a young man to play the lead role in a motion picture franchise. He must be athletic and

...

I got nothin'.

The casting decisions behind *The Last Airbender* movie make a clear, and clearly repugnant, statement:

Asian-American faces are simply inadequate for American audiences, even in a movie that so obviously celebrates our cultural heritage.

Look, I know how tiring it is to keep track of all the causes the modern world throws at us.

Paper or plastic?

Neither! I brought my own canvas bags!

But those are made by child labor!

And in the grand scheme of things, racism in the casting of a Hollywood popcorn flick, no matter how blatant, really isn't all that important. That's why I'm not asking you to picket or write letters or wear a T-shirt with a catchy slogan.

But if you want a T-shirt with a catchy slogan, Racebending.com has 'em!

I'm just asking you, especially on July 2, 2010, and the weekend after, to spend your entertainment dollars on something other than *The Last Airbender* movie.

Thanks for taking the time to hear me out!

Of all the things I've ever posted on the Internet, my *Airbender* boycott comic drew the most attention.

Look at all these comments!

Most of the comments were well reasoned and respectful, even when the writer didn't agree with me.

G!#?@!

Yikes!

Most.

One of the folks who read my webcomic was an editor at Dark Horse Comics. She got in touch.

So you're a fan of the *Airbender* cartoon, huh?

Yep. But not the movie.

Me neither.

Would you be interested in writing Dark Horse's upcoming *Avatar: The Last Airbender* graphic novel series?

Will the graphic novels have anything to do with the movie?

Nope. They'll continue the story from the original cartoon. They won't reference the movie at--

YES-I-WANT-THAT-JOB-RIGHT-NOW!!!

Moral of the story? If something bugs you about the world, say something. Do it respectfully and give good reasons.

Who knows what might happen?

TALENT SHOW

CHERRY CHEVA

Question: There are two high-school juniors in a room. They're waiting to audition for the talent show. One is an Asian girl. The other is a white guy. One is tuning a violin. The other fiddles with a scrap of paper containing notes for a stand-up comedy act.

Which one is which?

Yeah. I know what you'd say. That's what I'd say, too, except that I happened to be the guy. Holding the violin. On which I was about to play Fritz Kreisler's "Praeludium and Allegro." Hopefully in a non-sucky way.

And then there was the girl with the scrap of paper. She was tiny and cute and already sitting there when I walked in — we were the last two auditions of the day — and I knew who she was, though we'd never spoken. The last time I'd seen her was two years ago in personal fitness class, which is what they call gym at our school. It was usually taught by Mr. Choffley, a very, very in-shape gay guy who liked nothing better than calling his students fatties and mocking the contents of their lunch bags. But the semester I took it, Mr. Choffley was on sabbatical,[1] so we had Ms. Hain. She was normally just the chemistry teacher, and while she cared very much if you were wearing goggles while wielding a pipette of sulfuric acid in lab, she didn't give a crap what you did in personal fitness, as long as you were physically moving the whole time.

And so I spent a semester's worth of Tuesday and Thursday afternoons walking during fifth period. As did the girl who now sat before me. We'd both stroll lazily around the track, and since her pace was slower (*impressively* slower, actually) than mine, every once in a while I'd lap her. And nod as I did so. And get a nod back. We never had a class together again, but now here she was. Still tiny. Still cute. And there was nobody else in the room, and her audition wasn't for another eight minutes, and I was nervous as hell about my own audition, and when I'm nervous, I like to distract myself.[2]

Here went nothing.

"Hey," I said as I sat down. "Gretchen, right?"

She looked up at me, startled, and then I saw it slowly

1. We later found out it was a yoga retreat in the Bahamas called, for some reason, Agony & Ecstasy. It may not have been a yoga retreat.

register on her face. The register turned into realization, which turned into a smile. "Personal fitness," she said.

I nodded.

"Josh?"

Oh. She knew my name, too. I hadn't expected it. "Yeah. I don't think we ever introduced ourselves, but . . ."

"Yeah, I don't know, I just heard along the way or something. . . ."

"Yeah, same here."

"Yeah."

Silence.

"So what's your talent?" I asked. I couldn't discern it from looking at her.

"Well," she answered, pulling a scrap of paper out of her pocket and waving it in my general direction; I could see messily scrawled notes in purple ink. "I don't know if I have a talent for it yet. But hopefully it's, um . . . stand-up comedy."

The words were out of my mouth before I could stop them: "That's not very Asian."

She seemed amused instead of offended, thank God,

---

2. Because the alternative, which was what happened last year, is for my hands to get so sweaty that my bow slips right out of my fingers and breaks. My old bow cost six hundred dollars, so you can imagine how happy my parents were. My new one cost seventy-five on craigslist, and I had to drive all the way across town to pick it up, at some dude's garage that appeared to be housing a ferret-breeding facility, so you can imagine how happy I was.

raising an eyebrow as she glanced down at my violin. "Your talent isn't particularly Jewish."

Hey, look at that. She knew more about me than just my name and the fact that we'd had gym together. That was promising. "It's not *non*-Jewish," I pointed out. "Plenty of famous Jewish violinists."

"True," she agreed. "A non-Jewish talent would be, like, flashing some foreskin and then performing feats of strength."

I burst out laughing. "I hope that's one of your jokes."

"It isn't."

"Okay, well, tell me a joke, then. Do part of your act."

"No." She seemed almost horrified that I'd asked.

"Come on!"

"Hell no!" She crumpled up her notes and stuffed them back in her pocket.

"If you're too scared to tell one person, how are you gonna tell a whole audience?" Oops. Gretchen was now scowling. I had clearly crossed the line from "Hey, he's interested in my act, how flattering" to "Who is this belligerent dipwad, and would an uppercut or a right cross be the best way to punch him in the face?"

"That's completely the wrong logic," she snapped. "People laugh more when there's more people."

As if on cue, we suddenly heard muffled laughter through the audition-room door. "Who's in there?" I asked.

"Ballet dancer."

"Yikes." I pictured some girl twirling around and then falling on her head or something—although that probably wouldn't make the teachers running the auditions laugh. Kids, maybe. Me, certainly.[3] But not teachers.

"She probably just said something cute. Or did something cute. I heard them laugh when she first went in, too." Now we heard a smattering of applause, and Gretchen pulled out her paper again and started fiddling with it. "Okay, now I'm getting nervous."

"I've *been* nervous," I said. "Welcome to my hell."

"I'm pretty sure I'm gonna screw it up."

"Oh, you are not."

"No, I probably am." She said this very matter-of-factly, as if her voice wasn't concerned, but her hands sure looked like they were. They weren't shaking, they just looked . . . tense.

"So?" I asked. "What's the worst that could happen? Last year I was so nervous I dropped my bow and it broke." I'm third chair in the school orchestra, so it's not like I can't play in front of an audience, but the competitive aspect of auditioning makes normal performance butterflies into an entirely

3. Assuming no grievous injuries occurred. I, despite what Katie Finkelstein would tell you about a certain second-grade field trip to a working dairy farm, am not a monster. I had nothing to do with that cow kicking her in the head, although I did laugh; again, this was only because it was clear that she wasn't injured. Just hilariously humiliated. (Fine, seven-year-old me was sort of a monster. I've mellowed with age.)

different, well, animal. Butterflies on steroids. Butterflies with Uzis and anger-management problems.

"Oh, I'm sorry!"

"It's fine, I got a new one." I held up my bow. "Seriously though, if you don't make it, that sucks, but it's just a school show, right? And there's always next year."

Gretchen nodded. "Plus, if I do make it, I'd have to tell my parents." Her hands were now twisting the paper. It looked pretty ragged. I had doubts about its survival into the audition room.

"Well, yeah," I said.

"They wouldn't like it."

"Why not?"

She gave me a "You're kidding, right, you complete and total idiot?" look. "Asian," she said, gesturing at her face.

"What? I don't know your parents. Maybe they're progressive Asians. Maybe you're adopted."

"Nope and nope."

"Maybe once you get into the show and they come see you and see how talented you are, they'll change their minds and think their daughter doing stand-up is the most awesome thing in the entire—"

Gretchen rolled her eyes so hard I expected to have to chase them across the floor and give them to her to put back in her head.

"Okay, never mind," I said.

"I'm not even supposed to be here right now," Gretchen said. "They think I'm working on my science-fair project."

"So what *are* you gonna do if you get in?"

"Cross that bridge," she said darkly.

We sat in silence for a moment. I glanced at the clock and felt myself getting nervous again.

"Just tell me your opening line," I said.

"Oh, my God, I said no already! Why don't *you* play something for me, and *then* we can talk about whether I'll—"

I was already whipping through a four-octave G scale before she even finished her sentence. It turned out flawless. I hadn't expected it to, but somehow, channeling my nervous energy into talking to Gretchen (or goading her about her act) had calmed my fingers down. My left hand was no longer jumpy. My right hand was no longer oddly stiff. I finished with a flourish that was a hair too exaggerated, but I didn't bother to feel embarrassed because it's not like she was familiar with my playing style. For all she knew, I was normally that dramatic.[4]

"Oh. That was really good," she said.

"Thanks. I'm gonna assume your act is not, then, since you won't do it." I cocked an eyebrow at her. A dare.

"I don't have to take that from a Jew," she said. Her face

---

4. My style has actually been described by my teacher at various times as "staid," "stoic," "zombie-like," and "Did you take a Vicodin or something?"

was deadpan, her voice neutral, but her eyes were sparkling. A challenge.

"Whatever, slanty-eyes," I answered in an equally serious tone. "Go back to the rice paddy." I mentally winced in preparation for if it didn't go over well, but—

She burst out laughing, a sound like a bell, much more delicate than the tone of her regular speaking voice. I started laughing, too, and then the door opened. "Gretchen?"

Gretchen's face froze. She made a noise that was probably meant to be "yes" but came out more like a squeak, then got up and went inside. The door closed, and for the next five minutes, all I heard was excruciating silence. No applause. No talking. Certainly no laughter. She was either whispering her entire routine and they were whispering their appreciation, or she was bombing.

Bombing *big-time.*

I was suddenly very, very nervous again.

Another long, excruciating, silent minute as I stared at the wall clock, clinging tensely to my violin, silently fingering arpeggios up and down, up and down, up and down. Finally, the door opened and she came out.

"That went well," she said with an exaggerated gesture of both arms. It took me a second to realize that not only was she being sarcastic; she was also being sarcastic *about* being sarcastic, overemphasizing the fact that she was using a cliché. It took me another second to realize that I totally did not

have time to analyze the layers of somebody else's behavior right now. Because I was next.

My heart pounded. My hands shook.

"Do you wanna go out with me sometime?" I blurted.

Gretchen laughed. The bell sound again. The first laughter I'd heard in almost ten minutes. "Ha, thanks," she said. "Okay, I feel marginally better." Then she saw my face. "Oh. You're serious."

"Yeah," I said. My voice caught in my throat halfway through, turning the end of the word into a weird gurgle. Great.

No laughs now, just a smile.

"No," she said.

"Oh." I looked down at my violin.

"I don't want to be the girl who just, like, totally screwed up her thing and feels all bad about it, so then has to get a self-esteem pick-me-up from some guy asking her out, if that makes any sense?"

"Oh," I said. "Okay. I understand." I didn't understand. I didn't see how the two things were even related, but it didn't seem like pointing any of that out was going to endear me to her.

"Nice seeing you again, though!" She flashed me a grin and was out the door.

Dammit.

They called my name. I picked up my violin and went inside.

It was as silent during my performance as it had been during Gretchen's. I was once again very, very nervous. Sweaty hands. Shaking fingers. I didn't drop anything, but let's just say the number of times I messed up the first few phrases and asked to start over was more than zero. (It was six.)

But when I came out, Gretchen was back. Sitting there. Perched in the same chair she'd been in before.

"Okay," she said. "I changed my mind. Yes."

"What?" I asked, still shell-shocked from how truly badly I'd just screwed up. An hour of practice every day for the past month, and yet . . .

"Yes, I'll go out with you sometime," she said. "Uh . . . unless . . . you changed your mind. In which case forget it, forget I said anything—" She got up, blushing a little, and started heading for the door.

"What? No! No, I mean yes—I mean no, I didn't change my mind," I said, following her. "Uh . . . why did you change yours?"

"I can't tell you that," she said. "Asians are supposed to be inscrutable, remember?"

"I don't remember," I said. "I don't know what 'inscrutable' means."

That made her smile.

And I was so pumped up, I dropped my bow, which hit the floor and broke.

And Gretchen, that tiny, cute monster, that impressively slow walker, that possibly-bad-but-possibly-just-nervous-would-be-talent-show-stand-up, laughed and picked it up for me.

Voilà!

DEBBIE RIGAUD

When I was little, my great-aunt Ma Tante used to feed me breakfast. That was when she had a straight back—so long ago, I wasn't wearing glasses yet, if you can imagine. I must have been about three. My parents were at work, my big sister at school, so it was just Ma Tante and me.

As she dipped my bread in coffee, I got distracted by tiny particles floating in the beam of light entering the window above the kitchen sink. Ma Tante, ever vigilant of my feelings, asked what I was staring at. The peanut-butter-lathered bread I had been chewing stalled in the crook of my cheek. I pointed to the snowfall of particles. It seemed like the most magical thing I'd ever seen.

Ma Tante smiled. "Magical, *non*?" she asked, echoing my thoughts. "Things are always floating around us. But just like that sunbeam, it takes the light in our hearts to see magic that is invisible to most people."

From then on, wherever I went, I searched for magic around me.

"Voilà," Ma Tante would say to alert me to the tiny, every-day miracles in progress.

It was our secret.

I liked it better back when Tara and Tina were ignorant. Ever since the earthquake, this office's two medical assistants (or, as Ma Tante playfully refers to them, "the lookalikes") think they know everything about me. It's only been five minutes since my sister, Anne, dropped us off here, yet I'm already annoyed.

A sympathetic expression stretches the corners of Tara's eyes as she waits for my reply. She's taller and older than her sister.

"Yup—I'm fourteen now." I nod, squeezing the last bit of polite from my reserves. "And yes—*both* my parents are from Haiti."

"Oh, you see, TiTi?" Tara nudges her sister with the back of her hand. "I told you!"

I shrug. People have assumed this before—that I'm only half Haitian. Or at least, those who can't understand how a person with longer hair or lighter skin could come from Haiti.

My great-aunt is positioning her metal cane below her seat as she settles into her chair, getting acquainted with its contours in preparation for the long wait before her name is finally called. The doctor's office is filling up quickly. Over the past few years, as Ma Tante's painfully curved back has pulled her closer to the earth, the matching-scrub sisters started jumping her nearer to the top of the waiting list. But it's still going to take time. Lots of it.

"Go sit down, baby," Tara says, taking pity on me. "We'll call your auntie's name when the doctor is ready."

I harrumph to myself on my way to the empty seat next to Ma Tante. *When the doctor is ready.* I could bet any money he isn't even in. It never fails—halfway through our wait, the top of the good doctor's ample-sized dome can be seen bobbing past the driveway-facing window. He thinks he's sneaking in, but his conspicuously big head always gives him away.

Maybe it's because he serves the elderly. Or perhaps he's really Superman in disguise and there's always one too many emergencies going on at the local hospital. Whatever his story, Dr. Bighead's rarely in his office. Patients crowd the first floor of the converted old-time mansion that's rotting in the East Ward of our fair city. Waiting.

The one TV hanging precariously high in the corner is the waiting room's only timekeeper. Each program's theme song chimes the passing of yet another thirty minutes. From daytime talk shows to the evening news, they wait.

"Judge Judy's on," the large woman spread out over two chairs mutters to no one in particular. "Been here since *Good Morning America.*"

Ma Tante's done her share of waiting. She's been their patient—right word for sure—for over a decade. Some of my cousins are physicians, and I've heard them asking Ma Tante (on more than one occasion) to switch doctors. The old lady's too loyal to Dr. Bighead. She thinks he can do no wrong. But from where I sit, all he does is prescribe her more and more horse pills. And make her wait hours to be seen. Ma Tante doesn't speak English, so one of us waits with her. That is, until my older sister, Anne, learned to drive. The past few times, we've dropped Ma Tante off and popped in five hours later in time to translate her consultation. Not today, though. Anne dropped us *both* off, promising to be back minutes after we call her. I couldn't go home with her today because she said she had to go straight to a meeting. *Yeah, right.* Must be a really cute "study group" this time.

"*Sal' di?*" Ma Tante asks in Creole when I reach her. She wants to know what all the discussion with the lookalikes was about.

"*Rien,*" I respond respectfully—i.e., in French—as I was

raised to do when addressing an adult. I protect Ma Tante from the truth. It would hurt her to find out that, after all these years, the lookalikes have no clue that she is Haitian. Besides, Ma Tante thinks everyone adores her. And what's not to love? Most folks see this charming old lady with a peaceful gaze and a curved back and they have to restrain themselves from crouching down to hug her.

Ma Tante likes to flash her toothy smile and give away the only English offerings in her cherished possession. "Tank hyu," she answers, no matter what people say. Plus, Ma Tante treats Dr. Bighead's office like a nightclub. She dresses to the nines for her monthly appointments. Besides church, it's the only time she gets to go out these days. Today her flowery peach dress matches her hat, and she pulls an ornately embroidered handkerchief from her clutch purse.

"The lookalikes probably wanted to know where I've been," she says proudly, patting her forehead with the hankie. "They haven't seen me in a while."

"*Everybody* misses you when you're not around," I say.

She knows I'm teasing. "That's because they like how they feel about themselves when they see me," she says with that wisecracking tone in her voice.

"*Vraiment?*" I ask, a bit surprised that she's in the mood to talk. Ma Tante's obviously glad for my company—which makes me feel bad about sulking. Usually in public, she likes to keep the appearance of being a quiet, sweet old lady—not the hilarious, observant woman I enjoy being around. "Really? And why's that?"

"One look at my wrinkles, and they're excited they're not as shriveled up as me."

We tumble into a silent giggle. Me, shaking my head no and Ma Tante gesturing *oui*. But as messed up as it sounds, Ma Tante's probably right. Most people don't recognize the gems in front of them. And to me, Ma Tante is the most precious kind.

"That's not true, Ma Tante," I say, and rub her forearm, enjoying the easy movement of her loose chocolate skin. "You're a beautiful queen."

"Aaah, Simone." Ma Tante sings out my name in a delight that reveals she knew what I was thinking.

"Aaay, Simone?" This time my name rings out from a deeper voice. "Simone Thibodeaux?"

The first thing that catches my eye is his T-shirt. It's blue like his jeans, but with bright-orange letters that grab me. It reads CARE-A-VAN and under that, *Transporting Seniors to Caregivers.* The brain works superhero-fast. Quicker than an eye blink, I recognize the name of the volunteer group kids at my school sign up for in a frenzy to reach their monthly community service quota. Another millisecond later, my eyes dart up to the shirt wearer's face. What's Louis Milton doing way over in *this* part of town? He's from the West Ward.

"You're a volunteer here, too?" he asks.

"Um, no," I mutter, suddenly self-conscious. I clutch my phone. Why did Anne have to dump me here *today*?

"Oh," he says, and I can see he understands. *You're from the East Ward.* Before I can busy myself with a fake text, he continues. "Nice running into you, though."

I recognize that sympathetic look. I've seen it every time I have to turn down my friends because my parents won't let me go all the way to the West Ward at night. I hate that he feels sorry for me.

"Louis, help me out here, will you?" a girl calls from the front door. Oh, great. It's Waverly Webber from my history class. She's struggling to get an elderly man's wheelchair through the narrow entrance.

"Excuse me," Louis says to me before jogging over and pinning the heavy door wide open. Once Waverly and her senior are safely inside, Louis slips out.

"Gotcha here in one piece, Mr. P.," Waverly announces proudly.

Perhaps it's the piercing voice or the shift in the air brought on by Waverly's mere presence, but Ma Tante opens her heavy eyes wide and looks my classmate up and down.

"*Sal' yé?*" Ma Tante sings out under her breath, basically asking WTF (minus the F) in Creole.

Funny how Ma Tante picks up in Waverly what I do. The girl's actually never been mean to me or anyone else I know. It's just that her "Me first!" vibe can be off-putting.

This office never looked terribly low-budget to me before. But now, seeing Waverly here—her velvet red ballet flats stepping on aged, peeling linoleum floors—it's hard not to view things through her eyes. I suddenly feel exposed, as if Waverly just walked in on me getting my hair braided.

Good thing she doesn't notice me. Waverly's busying herself to our left, rearranging chairs to make room for her elderly companion's wheelchair. As she jams it into a narrow spot, the rush of the empty row of chairs slams Ma Tante's seat into mine.

Ma Tante reacts quietly. "Oh-oh?"

Mr. P. checks his neck for whiplash.

"There you *go*," Waverly tells him, smiling. She wipes her palms against each other and reports to the front desk in three quick strides. "I've brought Charles Pemberton for his three o'clock appointment."

If only Waverly knew that to Dr. Bighead, three p.m. means seven or eight p.m.

"Oh, and here's a list of medications that Mr. P. is currently taking," she says, not missing a beat.

"Okay, baby," Tina, the younger lookalike, says, taking the sheet from Waverly. "When the doctor comes in, we'll give this list to him."

The astonished look that takes hold of Waverly's face is priceless. "You mean he isn't here yet?"

Ma Tante pauses her humming to give a quiet chuckle.

"He'll be here soon enough," Tina says dismissively before heading toward the break room.

Perplexed, Waverly stops short of scratching her head when she spots me. "What're *you* doing here, Simone?"

"Hey, Waverly." I don't answer her question. This is my second chance to introduce Ma Tante, but I don't take it. I feel bad about that, but my embarrassment at being seen in the ghetto doctor's office outweighs the guilt.

But Waverly can't be shaken off the trail that easily. "Is this your grandmother?" she asks. Then to Ma Tante: "Hello, I'm Waverly — I go to school with your granddaughter."

"Mhmm. Tank hyu." Ma Tante smiles politely.

"She speaks Haitian?" Waverly asks, obviously tickled by Ma Tante's accent.

"Creole," I correct her. "And French."

Waverly finally asks her burning question. "So, you're here . . . even though you don't get any school credit for it?"

I nod. "I think they have new patient forms for the man you came in with," I say, counting on the fact that Waverly hates to miss a step.

It works. Her lips form an O, and she pads over to grab a clipboard.

Louis comes back, escorting a woman who walks with a cane. He looks so gentlemanly with his elbow extended for her to hold. A celebrated football player at school, Louis is taller and bigger than the average guy his age—so I'm mesmerized by how much he outsizes his companion.

The elderly woman lets go of Louis's arm and excitedly waves at Ma Tante. *"Koman ou ye?"*

"Oh!" Ma Tante sits up as best she can. *"Madame Bertrand, koman ou ye?"*

Louis seems touched by the women's gleeful greetings. His round face lights up like a stadium scoreboard at one of his home games. Despite his bulk, Louis is delicate with Madame Bertrand as he helps her into the seat next to Ma Tante's.

I get up to kiss Ma Tante's friend on the cheek. Even though I've never met her, doing so is customary. I stay standing. Here's my chance to redeem myself.

"Uh, Louis, this is my great-aunt, Ma Tante," I say.

Louis respectfully takes off his baseball cap and shakes Ma Tante's hand. He doesn't know about the cheek kiss custom, so he gets a pass.

"Janti ti gason." Ma Tante is impressed with him.

"Eh-heh." Madame Bertrand accepts the compliment as if Louis is her grandson.

"He would make a nice friend for my Simone," Ma Tante continues in Creole.

"I think so, too," replies Madame Bertrand.

"It's cute how they steal glances at each other, *non*?"

I can't hide my surprise, and Louis takes notice.

"What are they saying?" he asks me.

"Uh," I pause. "Just that . . . you're a well-mannered young man."

"Did he just ask you on a date, Simone?" Ma Tante is really trying to mess with me now.

"I'm going to have to separate you two," I answer, sassy in Creole.

The women giggle over Louis's confusion.

"I think they're saying more than that," he says, laughing and scanning all of our faces for clues. "C'mon, Simone, you're holding back."

"Simone, are you translating for Louis?" Waverly's finished Mr. P.'s paperwork and is drawn in by our laughter.

"Something like that," I answer, still blushing.

Waverly has an epiphany. "You can totally get credit for translating for Care-A-Van," she says earnestly. "Some Haitian seniors in the program need translators."

You know what? That could be cool. "That would be cool," I say.

"I'll introduce you to the program director, and you can get started right away," Waverly offers.

Funny that her persistence feels a lot more bearable when it benefits me.

"April Johnson?" Tara calls a patient to the back. Finally.

The large woman using two seats gets up, sighs heavily, and waddles to the exam room.

Immediately, Mr. P. rises effortlessly from the wheelchair and strides to nab the now vacant best seat in the house for TV viewing. We all look on in stunned silence.

"I told that chile I ain't need to be *wheeled* in," Mr. P. grumbles.

Ma Tante and I look at each other and burst out laughing. Louis, Madame Bertrand, and eventually even Waverly and Mr. P., cackle heartily with us.

"Voilà." Ma Tante winks at me.

I wink back.

THREE-POINTER

MITALI PERKINS

I have two gorgeous older sisters, but let the record stand: I was the first Bose daughter to score a point in the Game of Guys.

His name? Dwayne.

The place? A playground across the street from our Flushing, Queens, apartment, where I'd swing, slide, and ride my bike along with hordes of other immigrant kids.

The technique? Dwayne screeched his two-wheeler to a halt in front of mine, patted his Jackson Five Afro, and said, "Going to White Castle for lunch. Want to come along?"

Dumbstruck, I shook my head shyly and biked away.

I was nine.

Looking back, I should have eagerly accepted: "Yes, Dwayne, I'll go to White Castle with you. And then you're taking me to the prom in a decade or so, got that?"

It would be the only romantic invitation I'd get for years.

Soon after Dwayne made his move, our family left New York and settled in a San Francisco Bay Area suburb. I was in middle school, and my sisters were almost done with high school. Sonali, the oldest (her name means "gold" in Bangla), was a numbers geek, and Rupali ("silver") was an outgoing, leader-of-the-pack type. I came third ("friendly"—more valuable than precious metals in the long run, mind you), and my face was constantly planted in fiction. We Bose girls were nothing alike, but here's what we had in common: all of us liked guys. It was so much fun to watch, crush on, and, we hoped, date them.

The only problem was that we were the first Indians to move into this California neighborhood. In fact, we were the only folk of Asian descent for miles around. Also, there were no signs of any Afros like Dwayne's. The sea of whiteness didn't hinder my sisters—turned out plenty of Bay Area college dudes wanted tropical teen arm candy to complement their hippie lifestyles. Sonali and Rupali quickly ascended to expert level in the Guy Game.

Our parents knew nothing about this pursuit—they planned to arrange our marriages to suitable Indian men once we graduated with appropriate degrees in engineering or biology. Their ignorance was our bliss, we decided, especially when it came to dating. I kept my sisters' secrets, but I also secretly kept score. A sibling got one point if someone asked her out. A second if he gave her a compliment. A quick kiss won her a third. That's as far as I counted — going after a fourth point with the same guy would put my sisters in territory too dangerous to fathom. Heck, I figured if Baba caught them winning even one point, they'd be shipped to Kolkata and paraded before a bunch of parentally approved prospective grooms. Thankfully, Ma and Baba stayed out of the loop, and my sisters continued to accrue points right and left.

Sadly, when it came to me, Dwayne's invitation was still my only score. And it didn't seem like that was going to change too soon. At first, the other middle-schoolers in this born-in-the-USA neighborhood didn't know what to do with me. A few mumbled "hey" from a safe distance; most totally ignored my existence.

I didn't get why I immediately ranked so low on the social ladder, but in retrospect it's not hard to figure out. I would have crushed the competition in a Fresh Off the Boat poster contest. I was the whole FOB package — parents with lilting accents, super-strict father who didn't accept grades less than an A, house that perpetually smelled like turmeric and cardamom, ultra-traditional mother whose idea of party garb was six-and-a-half yards of silk *saree* and a forehead dot that mesmerized our neighbors. Plus, my skin was a color writers usually describe with food products like chocolate and coffee. At least *my* metaphors were addictive and tasty, right? I found it harder to define my classmates' hues in my diary.

They certainly weren't milky white, but "skin like deli-sliced turkey" didn't sound too appealing.

Surprisingly, the second time I gave myself a point in the game came after a few long weeks of peer-group silence. At lunch one day, a group of five geeks approached me. (You know the kind—precursors to today's *Lord of the Rings* fans who still collect Pokémon cards by the time they get to college.) My '70s geeks stood silently for a few minutes, elbowing one another to speak. One finally gathered his courage. "We need an Uhura," he told me. "We're heading to our usual spot over there. Want to come along?" The others nodded and waited eagerly for my answer.

I had no idea what they were talking about. After some questioning, I discovered these were Trekkies of a most intense type. They reenacted episodes of *Star Trek* every day in their corner of the cafeteria, each taking the role of a male character in the six-person cast. The sixth character in the show was a brown girl named Uhura, and it was clear (to them) that I'd been beamed down to repeat her few but important lines. I considered the invitation briefly—Spock was hot—before crushing their hopes.

The remainder of middle school involved episodes like a painful social dance class in PE, where I overheard a popular guy muttering about "fox-trotting with the Unibrow."

Mortified, I ran home to the bathroom mirror. Sure enough, my eyebrows were as impermeable as the fence between California and Mexico. My forehead was in San Diego, and my eyes were in Tijuana. My sisters found me in the bathroom crying over my hirsutism (look it up: excessive hairiness is a real diagnosis) and decided I needed help.

Rupali introduced me to eyeliner, tweezers, and a range of facial-hair removal strategies. Turned out American beauty products can take the South Asian right out of a girl.

Sonali excelled in science, so she told me about sex.

"You mean I won't get pregnant while using a public toilet?" I asked. That had been one of Ma's no-sex tips, filed under the broader category of "Avoid all contact with boys." "What about swimming at the Y?"

"Nope," my sister said. "The Y pool is pretty much baby-free. That is, if a girl keeps her suit on. Here, let me draw some pictures."

After digesting the facts of life as explained by my A+-in-biology sister, I pondered the miracle of our existence. Ma and Baba never touched in public or in front of us. The thought of either of them taking off any clothing was unimaginable. How in the world had the three of us been conceived through yards and yards of *saree* fabric?

My sisters' point totals were climbing, and I spied constantly on their dates (which usually started once the three of us were at the mall). I noticed two nonverbals that could come in handy if opportunity ever came my way: the Smoldering Look and the Hair Twiddle. Apparently, combining the two at the right time could seal the deal. I practiced for hours in front of the bathroom mirror.

Thanks to this intense sisterly schooling, I began to relax around guys. I even made some male friends by the time I started high school. These buddies confessed crushes on other girls in excruciating detail, and in return I offered advice gleaned from the adult fiction section of the library. Well-researched romance novels soon turned me into the school's number-one dating guru. I was at a suburban high school wearing jeans, not perched on a mountaintop in a white *saree*, but it didn't matter — scores of young men streamed to me for relationship advice.

No new points, though.

Meanwhile, my sisters suddenly stopped playing altogether. Thanks to a blossoming feminist movement on their college campus and a bunch of not-so-great experiences, they were now bemoaning time wasted with Stone Age chauvinists and losers masquerading as good guys. *Learn from our mistakes,* they warned me. *Wait for quality; skip the quantity.* I listened (sort of) but couldn't help thinking it was fine for them to quit, but I was still only at a grand total of two points. And did Dwayne's playground invitation and Spock's geeky move even count?

Then Steve moved into the neighborhood. He was a basketball star with strawberry-blond hair and blue eyes, so gorgeous that girls finger-fanned their faces when discussing him in the locker room. On his first day at school, I watched him open a door for a tottering, seventy-something history teacher, and *bam*, I was gone.

Steve turned up in most of my honors classes, and I put my best "I'm your buddy" foot forward. It worked superbly. After we shared a laugh or two, it was easy to add him to my coterie of guy friends. On the outside, that is. On the inside, I crushed on him madly, from freshman year until junior year. Nobody knew and nobody asked. I told the truth only to my diary, an orange notebook stashed deep in my desk.

By junior year, I was losing hope. There was no way Steve was going to like me. Not in that way, not a chance. I'd seen the vacancy in my male friends' eyes as they skipped across my face and body to scan a room for their white crushes. I did have the necessary feminine equipment, don't get me wrong, but apparently my body parts were the wrong hue to hold a gaze. In this neighborhood, they preferred deli-sliced turkey.

And then it happened. Steve stopped at our table on the way to eat with his basketball buddies. I was sitting with three of my friends, pretty Brady Bunch–ish blondes munching on PB & Js. Usually, guys talked to me with eyes fixed on my companions, but Steve was looking at me. Only me. And he was standing closer than any male buddy ever had. "Like roller coasters, Mitali?" he asked.

Swallowing the bite of leftover lentils and rice Ma had packed for me, I prayed he couldn't smell mango pickle on my breath. "Love them," I said, smiling brightly. *You've never ridden a roller coaster, you idiot. Don't lie to him!* "Love the idea of them, I mean. I've never tried one in real life."

"What?" asked Marcia, Jan, and Cindy in unison.

"Are you joking?"

"Don't they have roller coasters in India?"

Maybe they did. But we'd left before I had a chance to find out. Besides, life in a suburban American school felt like a crazy thrill ride that never ended. Who needed the real thing?

"You'll like the Giant Dipper," Steve said. "Our church youth group is heading to Santa Cruz on Saturday. Want to come along?"

Want to come along? I could hardly believe it — my dream guy had just joined the short list of dudes to ask me that question. First Dwayne, then Spock, and now . . . Steve. Apparently, I scored points only at lunch. "Sure," I said, deploying two years of finely honed "I'm your friend" acting skills to keep from shouting the word.

"We'll pick you up at noon," he said. "What's your address?"

"Sounds great," I said, lying again as I scribbled my address on a napkin. How would I explain a ginger-headed basketball player to my blissfully ignorant parents? Once again, I'd have to enlist my sisters' mad skills.

Steve tucked the napkin into his pocket and moved on. The girls at my table were quiet, but only for a bit. I watched them shake it off and start to chat about their weekend plans. This invitation was a blip, for sure. Guys asked *them* out in front of *me*, not vice versa. When it came to the scripts of their lives, I was the fourth chick, the one without a speaking part, the sidekick who never got her own backstory. I was starting to suspect I was only in the movie so the protagonist could add dimension to her character.

Saturday dawned, a breezy, summery, Santa Cruz–perfect day. I knew it wasn't a real date—there were a bunch of us going—but he had asked *me*, right?

"Are you sure this jock is worth it?" Sonali asked doubtfully.

Rupali chimed in. "Why's it taken him so long to ask you out?"

I didn't answer. My sisters exchanged glances and shrugged.

"Let's get you ready," said Rupali.

"What's our game plan?" asked Sonali.

I tried on eleven outfits before they finally agreed on the perfect combination—faded jeans, a white cotton shirt embroidered with flowers, and sandals with bling. Rupali convinced Ma to go shopping, Sonali asked Baba for help in chemistry, and I stole out to the porch to wait. My sisters were going to tell the truncated truth—I was spending the day at a park with some nice, studious friends.

The church ride was on time. I dashed to the curb and

jumped in before Steve had a chance to get out or Baba glanced up from Sonali's chemistry textbook. Acquaintances from school jammed the car, so no introductions were needed. We chatted with the others on the drive, but once we got into the amusement park, Steve led me away from the group.

"See you in a while," he told them, leaving a wake of confusion behind us. *Why does HE want to be alone with HER?* I could hear them thinking.

Before I could ask myself the same question, we were standing by the Giant Dipper. It was white, wooden, rickety, and huge. I gulped. "You'll like it—I promise," Steve said. "Just don't fight it."

He was right—I loved it. My head buzzed with the nearness of him as the Dipper twisted and turned us. That sweet old coaster kept tossing me over to Steve and hurling Steve over to me. We rode it three times, then crashed into each other's bumper cars, made crazy faces in the hall of mirrors, and shared fried dough. Steve swished a basket in the arcade and won an enormous stuffed monkey. He handed his prize to me with a smile sweeter than the dough we'd devoured.

"Let's name him Dipper," I said, swinging the huge creature onto my shoulders.

Steve reached over to brush the hair out of my eyes, and suddenly, it was time. I took a deep breath and hit him bang in the face with my best Smoldering Look. Oh, his eyes were blue, as blue as the California sky above our heads, as blue as the Pacific waves crashing on the sand. *Stow it,* I told myself. *Write the poem later. This is now, baby. Twiddle some Hair and keep Smoldering.* Oh, I Smoldered, all right. And Twiddled. All while balancing a monkey, no less—go on, try it, it's harder than it sounds—but thanks to my sisters' stellar training, I managed it.

During the ride home, Michael Jackson's "Rockin' Robin" may have been belting out on the radio, but my heart was dancing a crazy Bollywood dance. The only thing separating us was Dipper, one leg draped across Steve's jeans and one leg on mine. One by one the others were dropped off, but when it was just me and Steve in the backseat, he didn't move away. No, he stayed close, one denim leg pressed against mine. *To balance Dipper,* I thought. But then he wielded his own nonverbal. It was a classic guy move I'd watched college dudes use on my sisters: a yawn, a stretch, and suddenly an arm was stretched out across the seat behind me.

I knew the right response: lean in a little closer and clutch Dipper's paw.

The church car stopped in front of my house (*too soon, too soon*). I opened the door and swung out a leg. "Thanks so much," I said.

In a quick move, as smooth and agile as though he'd

practiced it a hundred times in front of a mirror, he leaned over and kissed my cheek. "You're sweet, Mitali," he said, and handed me the monkey.

And like that, he was gone. The car whisked him away, leaving me with points one, two, and three. I stood on the curb, squeezing Dipper so hard a real animal would have been asphyxiated in seconds. *So, that's the game,* I thought. *Hmm . . .*

The door opened. It was Ma, calling me inside, scolding about how late I was. I didn't care. I'd played the game; that was enough. But how was I going to explain the monkey business?

LIKE ME

VARIAN JOHNSON

"Griff, snap out of it," Evan says, jabbing his elbow into my rib cage. "You're missing the newbies."

I glance at Evan—trying to ignore the scraggly reddish-brown "soul patch" on his chin—then turn to follow his gaze. A mob of girls, huddled together like starry-eyed lambs heading to the slaughter, make their way across the quad with Principal Greer herding them along. With their blinding-white blouses and heavily starched skirts, they look like rejects from an episode of *Gossip Girl.*

Of course, my blazer and slacks would fit in the show just fine. As Principal Greer says, we're all cut from the same cloth here.

"Where are the boys? Did their group already pass?" Callie sports the same uniform as every other girl at Hobbs, but takes a more . . . generous interpretation on the skirt's length requirements.

"Did we look that scared last year?" Rebecca asks. "They're terrified."

Though talking to the group, she leans into me. I try to ignore the sweetness of her citrus-scented perfume, the color of her perfectly pink lips, the touch of her freckled hand against mine.

"Which one do you think'll bite the dust first?" Evan asks. "My bet's on the chubby one with the splotchy cheeks."

"No way," Callie says. "You see Tinkerbell—the one with the pixie cut? She probably still wets the bed."

Only a handful of events are certain at Hobbs Academy. The chicken enchilada will give you diarrhea. Coach Hawkins will mutter something inappropriate during the Spring Pep Rally and we'll all hear it thanks to the state-of-the-art sound system. And at least one freshman won't make it past the first two weeks. That last one may as well be chiseled in stone.

While Rebecca yells at Evan and Callie for being mean, my gaze falls to two girls at the tail of the mob. Rail-thin. Leggy. Dark-brown skin. Short, bouncy, black hair.

Twins? Maybe.

Black. Definitely.

I should know.

"What do you think?" Evan elbows me again, pushing me into Rebecca. "Which one leaves first?"

"The blonde," I mumble, trying to regain my balance.

"Which one?" he asks. "There are, like, twenty of them."

Exactly.

With about thirty students per grade, Hobbs is the smallest boarding school in Vermont. Our demographics are just like the state's. White, white, and white.

I guess that's not fair. Technically Rebecca is "one-eighth German, three-eighths Sephardic-Jewish, and one-half Irish." And Evan has enough Muskogee blood running through him to be a member of the Creek Nation. Still, I didn't see anyone looking at them when we talked about the Holocaust or the Trail of Tears last year in World History. But let anyone mention Dr. Martin Luther King Jr. or Will Smith or even the slightly black-looking dude who trims Principal Greer's prized rosebushes, and suddenly I'm the center of attention.

It got bad during Black History Month.

I own February at Hobbs.

Even the cafeteria lady gets in on it. Like: *I'm sorry, Griffin. So sorry. First—well, I'm sure I don't have to tell you, do I now?— we had slavery. Next came those horrible Jim Crow laws. And then Hurricane Katrina—can you believe it? Here, take an extra slice of cake. It's lemon. I've got watermelon and fried chicken and red Kool-Aid in back, too, just for you.*

(Okay, she didn't say all of that stuff. Not at the same time, anyway.)

But this afternoon in September, the cafeteria lady barely looks in my direction as she plops a scoop of lasagna onto my tray.

"Dude," Evan says as I near the table. "I heard there's twins in the new class. Twins!"

I slide into the chair beside him, bypassing the empty seat by Rebecca.

"They're in my PE class," Callie says. "Violet and Jasmine Harris. I think Coach is going to talk to them about playing volleyball."

"Volleyball-playing twins." Evan's eyes make him look like a rat in search of cheese. "How do they look?"

Callie glances at me. "You know . . . they're tall. And they have . . . brown eyes."

Evan's eyes dart around the room. "Yeah? And?"

"They're um . . . um . . ."

I drop my fork on the tray, not expecting the clang of metal on plastic to ring so loudly. "They're black."

The table falls silent. Another rule at Hobbs—no one talks about race. Like last year's mono outbreak and Principal Greer's BO, we ignore it—pretend it doesn't exist. Pretend it doesn't matter. "I saw them in the library." Rebecca picks at her salad—a sea of iceberg lettuce and creamy ranch dressing, with a few walnuts on top to make it reasonably healthy. "What makes you think they want to play volleyball?"

The question hangs in the air.

We remain statues.

Callie finally shifts. "They seemed interested in gym class." She tugs at the necklace around her reddening neck. "And I think I overheard them saying something about how they used to play at their old school."

The way she speaks, low and mumbling and more to the table than us, doesn't do her any favors.

Now it's Rebecca's turn to glance in my direction. "Callie, don't make stuff up." They've been friends since nursery school, so she never holds back.

I stare at her, and with my eyes I yell: *Control-Alt-Delete! Control-Alt-Delete!*

Rebecca doesn't get my silent code. But then again, she's a Mac type of girl. Those commands don't exist in her universe. "You thought they'd be good at sports because they're African-American. Admit it."

Callie shakes her head. "I never . . . Why would I—?"

I plaster the biggest smile I can muster to my face. "Like Callie would ever think something like that. You guys have seen me play basketball, right? Two-legged cockroaches jump higher than me."

They all laugh. Quietly. Politely.

Nothing like the way my cousins laughed when Benji cracked the same lame joke about me this summer.

Once everyone's provided the appropriate amount of laughter, we stuff whatever remains on our trays into our mouths.

Rebecca steals a few more glances at me but doesn't speak.

And Evan spends the rest of lunch talking about Tinkerbell.

So much for volleyball-playing twins.

The next day, right after calculus, I see the Harris twins coming down the hallway. Buds in their ears, heads bouncing. They're almost as tall as me, and I'm a hair under six foot.

I pause, letting everyone else slide past me out of class. When the twins are close enough, I try to catch their gaze, to give them a head nod — quick tilt back, chin up.

They keep walking. Don't even look in my direction.

Maybe they're too busy listening to their iPods.

Maybe they're too busy thinking about their next class.

Or maybe I just blend in with everyone else.

I see them a few other times over the next couple of days, sometimes in the hallway, sometimes in the caf, but I never have the opportunity to speak. I mean, yes, I *could* speak to them, but what am I supposed to say? *Hello, my Negro friends. Welcome to Hobbs Academy, which is whiter than rice and*

eggshells and vanilla-flavored milk. If you act like Bryant Gumbel
and Wayne Brady, you'll fit right in.

(My modification of yet another series of lame jokes
about me, courtesy of Benji. Uttered anytime I walked, spoke,
breathed, or blinked.)

So I don't speak to the Harris girls. And they don't speak
to me. We just pass each other, day after day.

It's quite possible that I could have gone on avoiding
Violet and Jasmine for another week, or maybe forever, if
Rebecca hadn't called me out.

"They asked about you," she says one Thursday night
when we're doing our homework in the study room on her
floor. Boys are allowed on the floor until eight p.m. I've been
here every night this week, even on days I didn't have homework. It's like I can't help myself.

"Who?" I ask, playing dumb.

"Violet and Jasmine."

"Oh. What did they want to know?"

"Just your name. Where you were from. If you were 'cool.'"

"Why'd they ask you?" I know the words come out harder
than they're supposed to, but I need to know.

"Violet thought . . ." Rebecca flips a page in her chemistry
book. "They see us together a lot."

We don't speak for a few minutes. I move on to my next
calculus problem, but I may as well be deciphering Sanskrit.

It doesn't help that Rebecca's wearing her hair like she did on our trip to New York last year. The drama club went to see *Wicked* on Broadway—and even though I was a set designer (well, more like a grunt for the set designer), I got to tag along. The play was okay, I guess. All I remember is Rebecca sitting beside me, dark curls spilling over her shoulders, skin smelling like oranges and mangoes, thigh pressed against mine during the entire show.

The musical was named right. There had been something wicked going on in my head. And in my pants.

"The young twin has a boyfriend," Rebecca says. "But not the older one. Not Violet."

"Um . . . okay."

Another flip of the page. "You know . . . in case you were interested."

I shake my head harder than necessary. "I don't like her," I say. Loudly. Just to be sure she hears me. "Not like that, anyway. I don't even know her."

Rebecca shrugs. Opens her mouth. Closes it. Shrugs again. Shuts her book. Takes a breath. "You said you were going to call this summer."

Her voice is low, and the hurt on her face slams into me harder than a thousand of Benji's lame, flat, painful, offensive jokes.

"I know. I'm sorry."

"Is it because . . . ?" Whatever bravery she exhibited confronting Callie on the first day of school has withered away.

"It's because I'm stupid."

We're both quiet. Rebecca's hair falls over her face, hiding her full, round cheeks. "You should talk to them," she says softly. "They're lonely."

Now it's my turn to shrug.

The next day I head for the library, hall pass in hand. Rebecca stands at the circulation desk but busies herself by looking in every possible direction except mine.

It doesn't take me long to find Violet.

At least, I assume it's Violet. They are twins, after all.

"Violet?" I ask, nearing the table.

She looks up from her textbook and slips the buds from her ears. "Griff. Wassup."

I sit down across from her. Her skin glows under the hard, bright fluorescent lights. "I just wanted to officially introduce myself. I've been meaning to, but—"

"Don't sweat it. I'm sure you got better things to do than hang with someone like me."

The sweat collecting underneath my arms approaches oceanic levels. "What makes you think that?"

"I'm a freshman. Low man on the totem pole."

"Sophomores aren't much better off," I mumble. "So where's your sister?"

Her smile falters. "In study hall, texting that sorry, trifling boyfriend of hers." She leans closer to me. She smells like aloe vera. Nice, but nothing like citrus. "I miss my boyfriend, too, but you don't see me moping around."

She has a boyfriend. I want to turn toward Rebecca and her dark curls and citrus-scented skin and yell, *She has a boyfriend!*

"It ain't just him. It's home." She strums the table. "She misses home."

"Hobbs takes a while to get used to."

"How long did it take you?"

I laugh. "When I get there, I'll let you know."

I'm in the middle of telling her about what cafeteria meals to avoid when Mrs. Whittaker walks over. The school librarian is out on maternity leave, so Mandy Whittaker's mom offered to substitute. Like an English degree, two snobby teens, and a huge bank account make you an expert on all things literary.

"You two getting any work done?" Mrs. Whittaker asks.

"Griffin was nice enough to come over and introduce himself. He's giving me some pointers about school."

She glances at Violet's notebook. "What are you studying?"

"English." She moves her hand, giving Mrs. Whittaker

full view of her notebook. "I'm working on an essay on *I Know Why the Caged Bird Sings*. By Maya Angelou."

"I'm familiar with the book," Mrs. Whittaker says, touching the top button of her blouse. "I thought your class was reading *The Book Thief.*"

"By Markus Zusak. I read it last year." She doesn't blink an eye. "Mr. Brooks and I thought it would be more worthwhile to focus on another book."

"I see." Mrs. Whittaker's voice is different. Smaller. She looks around the table, letting her eyes settle on the open Angelou book. The pages sport an assortment of highlights and underlines, with notes in the margins.

"It's my personal copy," Violet says.

"Of course." Mrs. Whittaker nods to Violet, then to me. "Let me know if I can help, okay?"

After Mrs. Whittaker leaves, Violet shakes her head. Her eyes remind me of a dull penny. "Sorry 'bout getting you into trouble. My bad."

It's almost magical, the way she switches talking like that.

Some people call it slang.

Teachers call it bad English.

Idiots call it Ebonics.

And me—I call it just talking. Like you do with family.

I want to be like her, loose and carefree with my vowels and consonants, right here at Hobbs. Because lately, even at home with my cousins, the words are starting to come out stiff and broken and wrong. The last time I was home, they said I sounded white.

I shake this thought away. "I'm not worried about Mrs. Whittaker."

"That ain't who I'm talking about."

I look back toward the circulation desk. Rebecca is scrubbing the counter with a dust rag. I can almost see the varnish rising from the counter, and the steam rising from her head.

"She don't have anything to worry about. Like I said, I have a boyfriend." She glances at Rebecca. "She's nice. Everybody thinks you two would make a nice couple."

"Really?" I ask. "Everyone?"

The way she looks at me, I know she understands what I'm trying to ask.

"Don't date her if you don't want to. It's a free country. But she's got it bad for you. And from the way it sounds, you're jonesing for her, too."

That's all she says. No jokes about the other white meat. No teasing about the black man's kryptonite. No jabs about Mr. Oreo looking for a glass of milk.

She picks up her earbuds. "I'd better get back to work. This essay ain't going to write itself."

I take a scrap of paper and scribble my number on it. "Just in case you need to get ahold of me. About anything."

She takes the paper. "Hey, whatcha got going on this weekend? Want to hang out with me and Jazzy on Saturday? It might take her mind off of home and that sorry boyfriend of hers." She pops her knuckles. "I've been waiting for the right time to bring out the dominoes. And now that we have a third player . . ."

I think about lying or coming up with some excuse, but after the conversation we had, Violet deserves better. "I don't know how to play."

She blinks twice, like she's processing the data. "Oh. Okay. We'll teach you."

I sit there, not sure what to say.

She's already got her nose back in her book. "And if you want, bring Rebecca. That way we can play spades, too."

I head to circulation, which smells of wildflowers and ammonia. And oranges and mangoes. "Thanks for getting me to talk to Violet."

"No problem. I forgot you guys were even in here."

Sure she did. I reach across the wide desk and place my hand on hers. Mrs. Whittaker would have a heart attack if she saw, but who cares? "What are you doing for lunch?"

She glances at my hand. "You don't want to go to the caf with Evan and Callie?"

"No. Let's walk over to Pat's."

"Just us?"

"Yeah. Just us. Like we used to last year."

She gives me a smile that grabs me and refuses to let go. "You're buying."

I squeeze her hand, smile one last time, and head for the exit. Right before I open the door, I look back at Violet and give her a head nod.

She sees me, and she nods back.

Confessions of a Black Geek

OLUGBEMISOLA RHUDAY-PERKOVICH

In high school, my friends and I owned two words — we were Black, and we were geeks. We had the soundtrack to prove the first: classic Nina Simone and Aretha Franklin renditions of "Young, Gifted and Black." That song was as much a part of my regular diet as the lumpy and not-sweet-enough porridge I had for breakfast many mornings. My mom was an Excellence for Black Children mother, which meant that she battled for Parent-of-a-High-Achiever supremacy at monthly meetings and was quick to whip out the dashiki and boom box so that I could dance interpretively alongside my equally gifted and well-mothered friends at the annual Martin Luther King Jr. breakfasts.

We were on display at family gatherings, too — some evil auntie or uncle got the idea to have "the young people" perform every Thanksgiving before dinner. If we did not slouch to the center of the living room to recite a little Langston Hughes or perform a painful excerpt from our last piano recital, we could forget about eating. My cousins and I grumbled and threatened revolt, but . . . miss out on more codfish cakes and mac and cheese? We performed.

But let's be honest. My friends and I didn't need *that* much prodding to put excellence on display, especially the academic variety. We were serious geeks. Second proof: we voluntarily joined (and were the only members of) the math and debate teams. We brought *all* of our textbooks home daily (just in case) in book bags the size of igloos. K. and I would call each other breathlessly on report card day to tally our As and A+s. (It was understood that the occasional B was too devastating to discuss.) We took such excessive pride in our academic achievements that when K. received an A instead of an A+ with a 98 average, we hurried to Mrs. H. to rectify this grievous error, with me along as his consigliere. Maybe Mrs. H. had gotten confused?

No. The A would stand, "because you're pompous," she told us.

Okay, so Mrs. H. wasn't confused. But clearly she needed a sabbatical.

Looking back, though, Mrs. H. might have been onto something. K. and I *were* certain that our all-around fabulosity knew no bounds, and certainly not racial ones. Our high school was an oasis of suburban racial integration. These were the '80s; "Ebony and Ivory," Stevie Wonder and Paul McCartney's pop hit of the era, could have been our school song. Jheri-curled and Sun-In'd hairstyles were equally welcome at the best parties. Our school put on *The Wiz* with a multiracial cast, and when we did *The Crucible*, the drama coach was sensitive enough to ask the Black members of the troupe if we'd be uncomfortable playing the role of slave Tituba. "Ummmm . . . yeah," I murmured, imagining my mother's face if I'd dared to come home saying, "Hey, Mom! I'm going to play the slave in the school play! Invite the whole family!" She would've thought I'd lost my mind.

Still, I was secure enough in my two-word identity to wear different personas like the rubber bracelets that snaked up my arms. In playwriting workshop, I explored my younger days of dancing on the bed with a "blond" towel on my head in a thoughtful piece; after school, I giggled through the mall talking like a Valley girl with friends of every shape, size, and hue — we were like piano keys, melodious and harmonic, dancing to the same beat of mutual respect. We acknowledged the chocolate-and-peanut-butter perfection of Aerosmith and Run-D.M.C on "Walk This Way." Smurf was both TV noun and dance-party verb, and Prince vs. Michael Jackson? Stumped us all. Just when *Thriller* and the moonwalk took our collective breath away, *Purple Rain* stormed in, wearing high-heeled boots and rolling pop, rock, heavy metal, and

R&B into a glorious ball of awesome. Black and White, we all loved the spare beats and synthesizers of '80s music (and the hair! Have you *seen* the *hair*? Seriously, google it. I'll wait.).

So of course, my friends and I were sure our White classmates weren't *racist*. Racists were red-faced people wearing white sheets. They were not sitting next to us in AP English or competing with us for the Individual Research Projects in Science Award. We giggled and got good grades alongside one another, we were on the honor roll together, and we collectively celebrated the rise of hip-hop and blue-eyed soul.

But surface harmony notwithstanding, there were cracks in the veneer.

When I proudly displayed one of Keith Haring's giant Free South Africa posters in my room, a friend came to visit and went white with outrage (pun intended). "That poster seems like it's saying the Black people should rise up and crush White people," he said. "They should really *try talking to them first.*"

Of course.

The nearly fifty years of resistance to the government system of apartheid could not have possibly included some talking.

Even the music we shared started to feel a bit offbeat. As much as I admired the philanthropic sentiment, some of the lyrics in "Do They Know It's Christmas?" the star-studded musical call for famine relief in Ethiopia, made me squirm.

At school assemblies, the whole student body rapped and sang along to "Caravan of Love" and "King Holiday," but the ugliness of Howard Beach, where a group of Black men were chased by a mob of White men through the streets of New York City and severely beaten, was only minutes away.

My visits to the school library stopped after I'd asked the librarian where I might find resources for my research paper on Zora Neale Hurston and she told me there was "no such person."

Oh-kayy...

Whatever. I had work to do. I was getting ready to move on to college, where surely more enlightened adults waited to affirm my brilliance. Pompous, that's right.

Then the school newspaper published a cartoon featuring Black teens speaking "Ebonically" ("Dat's nasty!"). My friends and I (also on the newspaper staff) were not amused. Accompanying the cartoon was an op-ed of sorts decrying "Black" behavior at parties, and Black students drafted and signed a petition condemning the piece. We were at first buoyed by the number of student allies who immediately expressed their support. But things got sticky when those allies wanted to add their names to the petition, and we held fast to the notion that a petition from "We, the Black students" should be signed by . . . well, *the Black students*. It went back and forth. Feelings were hurt. We held our ground, suggesting that sympathetic parties start another petition, add a rainbow coalition of outrage to the voices of protest. That didn't go over so well. We were called "reverse racists." The principal called me into her office and gently asked that as student body president, I lead the charge to amend the petition so that White students could sign it. I declined politely. Later that day, the newspaper advisor explained to me and a friend that it was one big misunderstanding and had not been done to offend and oh-so helpfully added that in her day, minstrel shows were legitimate entertainment. The newspaper editors, genuinely chagrined, issued an apology, and life went on. Or so it seemed.

After the school newspaper incident, my friends and I were no longer at ease, but the discomfort was muted by empowerment lessons imparted by our parents and people like Ms. B., who shared both Oprah and Okonkwo (of Chinua Achebe's *Things Fall Apart* fame) with us in African history class. There was Ms. Z., who had the vision and authority to ~~shove~~ nudge us into extracurricular Black theater. I played Mama in *A Raisin in the Sun* (my chagrin at having to play an "old lady"—with padding!—barely mitigated by the fact that I'd gotten a lead role), and yes, we revisited the dashiki days to dance interpretively to Claude McKay's poem "White Houses" in front of the entire school. We were frequently mortified, but more often filled with confidence and pride. We took pride in knowing our roots (and how to dramatize them), and since my friends and I were a competitive group in a competitive class, the A+s flowed. We envisioned ourselves easing on down the road to a top-tier-college future.

I had a pretty good portfolio of College Material that could open doors at a variety of hallowed halls named after Rich Dead Guys. Here I was — honor roll? Check. Good SAT scores? Check. More activities than I actually had time for? Check. I once calculated my after-school commitments and the time that each needed, and it came out to just under sixty-six hours a week. And that was before I counted weekends. Let the record show that I was undeterred. As a reader of both science fiction and fantasy, I figured it was only a matter of time before I uncovered the secrets of time travel, transmogrification, and magic wardrobes that would allow me to Do It All. Looking at the "me" on paper, how could I not expect to be a desirable candidate in the world of higher learning?

And then I signed up for my first and only college prep meeting with my guidance counselor. He took one look at my list — Northwestern, University of Pennsylvania, Cornell, and SUNY Binghamton — and smiled a smile that didn't quite reach his eyes as he said, "These schools are kind of a reach for you."

A reach? For *me*?

I was a certified, bona fide, flag-waving geek. I assumed it was generally accepted common knowledge. Giving him his smile right back, I left the office feeling a little sad for this man who so obviously didn't know Whom He Was Dealing With.

Growing up with Maya Angelou and Malcolm X, Sweet Honey in the Rock, Black History Month every month of the year in my home, and a rainbow coalition of friends and family meant that I *knew who I was.* (I knew who Zora Neale Hurston was, too.) And where I should apply to college.

I waited for the acceptance letters to roll in.

And they did. For all of us. We wore our status like the alligators emblazoned on our shirts. We were academic superstars, remember?

Apparently, not everyone did. At least, not many of our counterparts remembered that we were the same people who sat next to them in AP classes, occasionally gave homework help, and assisted in decoding the poetic genius of hip-hop's pioneers. When the news spread about our acceptances, all of that didn't matter anymore.

We lost one of our labels just like that.

Suddenly, we were no longer part of the school's elite geekarati.

We were only very, very Black.

"It's just . . . so *wrong*," sputtered my Don't Free South Africa acquaintance on the phone, who was now more well versed in the nature of injustice. "It's *not fair*. Someone like E., who's worked so hard and is so smart, gets rejected from

Harvard, but all of these Black people get into Ivy League schools."

Excuse me?

"People like me, you mean?" I said sweetly, ever polite. My mom taught me manners, even in the face of extreme jackassishness.

There followed much stammering and blustering, and assurances that, of course, he hadn't meant me.

I realized then and there that the same people who'd asked for my notes were always going to see me as more C– than A+, no matter what the report cards said or how good my notes were. And their parents, grumbling about affirmative action and lowered standards in the same breath, probably fed them those thoughts at the dinner table. And some of the wonderful teachers who quietly but fiercely looked out for us let us know that some of their colleagues felt that way, too.

It broke my heart.

I thought I knew the face of racism. In second grade, a classmate who knew a lot of bad words and very little about personal space followed me daily murmuring *"Nigger-niggernigger"* in my ear. Yeah, that was A Year to Remember. And then there was the way our community welcomed an interracial couple — with a cross-burning. Thankfully, a number of neighbors had led a march and vigil in objection to that heartbreaking display of ignorance.

Now I looked around our school and wondered, "Are *you* like *those* cross-burning, epithet-spitting people?"

My teachers and classmates *knew* me. And still the answer to my question wasn't clear.

It. Broke. My. Heart.

But it didn't take long to open my eyes and see the truth: *It was their problem.*

If they didn't get it; well, that was too bad.

I wasn't going to *try talking to them first.*

I'd gotten into the colleges of my choice because I'd worked every multidimensional bone in my body to get there.

I didn't need to be in AP Bio to know how wrong it is to be reduced and flattened to a color (but I was). I wave my identity flag high and wide, marching-band style (yep, did that, too — polyester uniform and all).

I'm Black. I'm a geek.

And nobody can divide that beautiful partnership.

Under Berlin

G. NERI

Berlin is like a theme park.
You got your Nazi Land —
with its huge war monuments,
stone eagles staring you down,
and gold bricks in the ground
telling you how many Jewish folks
from your building died in the war.
You have your Commie World,
all gray and rectangle blocks
of boring buildings,
old Karl Marx statues,
and leftover parts of the Berlin Wall
standing next to a Starbucks.

Then you got Futurama,
where you can ride around on those weird
Segway people movers,
zipping past gleaming towers
and lit-up pyramids
(like Las Vegas but more classy),
all built in the empty space
where the Wall came down.

It's all interesting, I guess.
We're only here
a year for Daddy's work,
so I can put up with anything—
even starting high school
in a place that never heard of
homecoming.
What makes it okay is the food.
There are these amazing gelato stands
(only eighty cents a scoop!),
bakeries on every corner with sweets
you wouldn't believe,
and the currywurst—
that's bratwurst with curry ketchup—
man, I could eat that *forever*.
I'm thinking of opening
a chain of my own

when we get back to the States.
It's that good.

But there are things that suck, too.
German is *hard,*
and nobody ever smiles and says,
Hey, wassup, girl?
When it's cold,
everybody seems grumpy —
I guess complaining about winter
must be like a national sport here.
And then there're the subways. . . .

Me and my family head down
the subway stairs
past the stone eagles
and homeless musicians,
past the currywurst stand
where we usually get a snack.
No stopping today,
it's wall-to-wall
people —
all Germans —
tall and pale,
towering over me
like Euro-gods with tiny glasses.

"Why can't we take a taxi?" I ask.

"You all gonna pay for it, Reina?" asks Daddy,
his southern twang
more out of place
than we are.

We move slowly across the platform,
pushing into the overcrowded train car.

"Sure, I'll pay,
just as soon as I start my own
currywurst stand."

I can still smell it from here.

My brother, Oscar, laughs. "Yeah, right."

I stare at his pudgy face,
trying not to get squished
by the rush-hour stampede.

"What's so funny?" I say.

Oscar laughs again.

"A black American girl
servin' up German sausage?
Sure, that's not funny
at all."

"I'm not *black*," I say.

An old punk rocker,
all leather and tattoos,
laughs when I say that.

I shoot him a look.

My dad is black,
in a real southern way.
But Mom is a light-skinned Hispanic
from Puerto Rico,
so I'm as black as Obama, I guess,
which is only half.
My bro rolls his eyes. "Sorry.
I meant '*mixed* American.'"
His eyes light up —
"Or how about '*mixed-UP* American'?"
Mom makes a face.
"That doesn't even make sense, Papito."
Oscar shrugs, like she ain't
hip enough to get it.

The doors start to close,
so I give Oscar one last shove
'cause we still sticking out
the train door a bit.
We make it in
as the doors seal shut,
but now he's squashed up
against a pole,
looking like he wished
he didn't have a sister.
"You should thank me

for saving your butt," I say.
"You coulda got cut in two
by them doors.
I heard it happened once."
He's thinking of a comeback.
"I pretty sure your *big* butt
woulda stopped those doors
from closing," he mutters.
I laugh in his face. "Dude,
so weak. Move on
before you embarrass yourself.
Oops, sorry, too late."
Then we ignore each other,
standing like sardines
in a tin can with windows.

Mom's feet ache.
So do mine.
Too much walking here,
not like in the States.
Guess that's why
they ain't all fat here.
All they do is walk
and take the subway,
or the *U-bahn,* as they call it.
I wish we had a car,

but Daddy says the subway
is a good way to
"mingle with the people."
That's the only way
to get into a strange culture,
he says — dive in,
headfirst.
So we ride them,
morning
to night.
No taxis for this *familia.*

The subway's kinda like
watching reality TV —
you see all kinds.
I've seen the clothes change
from season to season since we got here:
shorts and porkpie hats and flip-flops
in summer
become heavy coats and fur caps and boots
by winter.
There's funny-looking people:
hipster artist types trying to act all Euro-cool,
workers reading big ol' novels,
students bopping to their iPods,
tourists looking lost and confused.

But most of all,
old people.
Lots of 'em.
I don't think I ever seen
so many old people before.
Daddy says they ain't that old—
they just look it.
Ex-Communists
who lost their way of life
when the Wall came down.
You'd think they'd be happy,
but the older ones aren't.
They like making your life
miserable
'cause they can't have it their way
anymore.
Daddy says, *Just kill 'em
with kindness.*
But they never smile
or give *us* the time of day.

Daddy looks around for a place
to park our butts.
The train is jam-packed—
no place to go.
But he smiles,

winks at me,
and nods toward
two older women,
all uptight with little glasses
and what they think passes
for style: beige pants, beige jackets,
colorful scarves,
and poofy colored hair.
To me, it seems
they all dress the same,
like they in the same old people's club
or something.
There is one empty seat
between them.
Or at least
Daddy thinks there is.
It's more like a small gap,
but it'll do.
"Honey, it's *on*," he says,
pointing to their row.
"Not funny, Papi," Mom says,
frowning.
I look at the old ladies,
especially the one
with a bright-red mop of Lola hair
who holds a small dog

as sour as she is.
I laugh. "Good luck with *that.*"

Daddy shrugs. "I didn't invent the rules.
I just play the game."
"Some role model," Oscar pipes in,
taking Mom's side.
"Mama's boy," I say.
"Daddy's *girl,*" he says, all cutesy
'cause he knows I hate that.
Daddy puts his hands
on our heads.
"Y'all missed
the freedom-bus protests,
so you have no idea," he says.
Mom clears her throat.
"Papi, you were two years old back then,"
she says, blowing his cover.
Daddy gives her a look and shrugs.
"Just sayin'. Now, let your man
go to work."
He adjusts his tie,
smooths down his goatee,
and heads toward the two old ladies,
all smiles and southern charm.
He tips his invisible hat

and says in his best Alabama-German,
"How y'all doin', *fraw-lines*?"
then motions to the empty spot.
They grimace,
like they just swallowed
something bad.
"*Dan-ka*, ma'ams," he says politely,
not waiting for an answer.
He wiggles between them,
clears his throat,
and waits
for the next move. . . .

I try to make eye contact
to see if I can make him
laugh.
But he doesn't.
He has on
his most saintly face,
like he just got baptized
by the pope.
The ladies are
squirming on either side of him.
Even the dog
is jumpy.
It's like Daddy has a disease

or something.
They're looking around,
trying not to be too obvious
about their discomfort,
but he can't help but rub shoulders
with them.
My guess is they watch
American TV and think
if you sit next to a black man,
it's only a matter of time
before he robs you.
Even if he's wearing a suit,
he could still be one of those
Malcolm X brothers.
Ach, mein Gott!

It's like watching popcorn
pop—
sooner or later
they're gonna blow.
I look at my watch.
Thirty seconds.
Mom catches my eye,
frowning at our game.
I ignore her like I don't know
what she's on about.

It used to bother me
when we first arrived in Berlin.
I mean us getting on the subway.
I know these folks
can't quite figure us out.
Daddy's dark skinned;
Mom's light tan.
Oscar looks like a white boy.
But me, I look like an overcooked
mini Jennifer Lopez with nappy hair.
Back home, we ain't no big thing.
But here, they don't know
what to think.

I think Daddy made up
this game,
to show us not to sweat it —
it's all a big joke.
We're doing
social experiments is all.
"See, America's an immigrant country,"
he told us when we first got here.
"We're used to rubbing shoulders
with all kinds.
But here,
they *never* had immigrants

until recently.
They're just *now* learning. . . ."
Not so well,
as far as I can see.
When the Germans brought the Turks
over to do all the manual labor jobs
fifty years ago,
they probably didn't think
Berlin would turn into
the third-largest Turkish city
in the world!
Seems they're sorry
they opened *that* door now.

"Hey, pup, what's your name?"
Daddy's trying to make nice
with the little mutt
in the red-haired lady's lap.
It growls back.
The lady shushes it,
but when Daddy tries to pet it,
she pulls her dog away
and looks up at the announcement board,
like her stop is coming.
She struggles to get to her feet,

then makes her way
to the door,
out of Daddy's sight.
But I keep my eyes on her.
When she thinks
he can't see her anymore,
she spots an empty seat
and slides in next to a nice-looking
German couple.

Daddy spreads out a little more,
his elbow almost touching
the other lady.
He makes eye contact
with me.
I stick my tongue out,
thinking just one
don't count.
If you can't clear out seats
for all of us, then—

Suddenly, the other lady
takes out her cell phone
and acts like it just rang.
Pretends

she can't hear
and has to get up
to walk to another part
of the train for better reception.
But I happen to know
the phones don't work
down here.
Least mine don't.
Still, she gets points
for her acting.

Daddy smiles
and waves us quickly over.
Mom disapproves
but is too tired to argue.
He stands as we squeeze in,
grateful to be sitting
after all that walking.
"Under a minute —
that's pretty good," he says, leaning over,
waiting for my concession speech.
It ain't coming.
"That last one
should become an actor —
she got mad skills," I say instead.

Me and him crack up,
even as a couple across from us
listens in.
I know they know what we're saying,
but I'm just gonna pretend
they don't.
"People here
sure like to move about,
don't they? These seats
must be bad
or something."
I fiddle with mine,
like it's broken.

Mom frowns again.
"I wish you two wouldn't do that.
If this was Montgomery
or Selma in the sixties,
it wouldn't be so funny,
would it? Back in Puerto Rico —"
Daddy cuts her off. "You sitting,
aren't you?
That's like some southern kung fu move —
take all that bad energy
and rechannel it to advance

the cause."
Mom doesn't buy it.
"I'll give you kung fu, Papi," she says,
holding up her hand
to his face.
But he just smiles
that grin of his,
the one that always
melts her heart.
She shakes her head and
finally cracks a smile, too.
Next thing you know,
he leans down and
they kissing.
How can they do *that*
in public?

We sit for the longest time,
making our way across
Berlin.
Turks are starting to board,
and some of the Germans
get off.
When those two ladies
bust a move for the door,

I smile and wave,
even though they ain't looking
my way.
"See ya next time!" I call out.
Mom playfully slaps my hand.
"Stop it. They can't help it
if your Papi is so handsome
it hurts to sit next to him."
Dad pats his hair
and throws us a grin.

Now a couple of Muslim girls
in head scarves sit next to me.
I gotta admit,
it makes me feel weird,
them having to cover up an' all.
Mom notices my face.
"Want to move?" she whispers.
That's what she likes to call *irony*.
I don't play that game.
My brother leans over.
"You might look good
in one of those scarves, Reina.
Especially the ones
that cover your face."

I take the high road
and ignore him.
Mom's impressed.

Another ten minutes pass
and I look around.
No Germans left—
mostly Turks,
Chinese,
Vietnamese,
Africans,
and us.
They all smiling,
looking around like *this*
is how
it should be.
Talking and laughing,
dancing to a Greek guy
playing his crazy violin for money.
They all just biding their time,
waiting for the Europeans
to accept them for who they are.
But things are changing,
a little too fast for some
and way too slow for others.
But someday,

they'll see:
sometimes
you just gotta squeeze your way in,
rub some shoulders,
and hope
they'll rub back.
For that,
I'd be willing to stand.

Just not next to my brother.

Brotherly Love

FRANCISCO X. STORK

The day I talked to my sister started out as an ordinary Sunday. Papá began yelling at us to get ready two hours before we needed to leave for church. I knew Rosalinda would be staying home because I had heard her battle with Papá earlier that morning. Once a month, Papá reluctantly agreed to let Rosalinda stay home on account of *problemas de mujer.*

"Luis, let's go!" I heard Papá yell all the way from his room. I covered my face with my pillow.

"You all right?" Bernie was standing over my bed. He had a worried look on his face. He and I had shared a room since forever. "You haven't been yourself lately. Is everything okay?"

It was hard to keep things from Bernie. He could read something wrong a mile away. And when he asked how you were, it was difficult not to spill your guts out. But there was no way I could tell him what was bothering me that particular morning. Rosalinda was the only one that could help me.

"I can't go to church today," I said.

"Why?" Bernie asked. "Aren't you feeling well?"

"I just need to stay home — that's all."

Bernie was thoughtful for a few seconds, and then he gave me this look as if he understood that my problem was more mental than physical.

"Luis! Why aren't you up yet? We're late!" Papá's large body seemed to fill up most of the room. He had on his shiny black suit with the usual fully starched white shirt and the blue tie with velvet stripes that our mother had picked for him when she was still alive. On Sundays Papá always reminded me of an undertaker. Papá placed his hands on his hips, and that was the signal for me to get up. I never argued with Papá once he put his hands on his hips.

"Papá," Bernie said softly but firmly, "I think Luis should stay home."

"What's the matter with him?"

I glanced at Bernie and then at Papá. "I'm okay," I said.

"He's sick," Bernie said. "He was up all night coughing." I could have sworn I saw Bernie wink at me.

"I didn't hear nothing," Papá said authoritatively.

"Besides, since when does a little cough keep a real man from doing what he needs to do?"

I glanced up at Papá's face in the hope that he might be joking. But no, when it came to pronouncements on what real men do, Papá never joked.

Bernie was not giving up. I don't know how he did it, but he had mysteriously figured out how important it was for me to stay home that morning. "If Mamá was here, she'd make him stay." I was standing up now. Bernie reached out and placed the palm of his hand on my forehead. "Go ahead and touch him," he said to Papá. "He's burning up."

Papá lifted his hand slightly as if to touch me and then changed his mind. "Both of you guys are a bunch of girls, I swear." Papá waved his hand in disgust. "Go ahead and stay, if you're so sick."

We waited until Papá was out of the room. "Thanks," I said to Bernie.

"Enjoy," he responded.

My sister's bedroom shared a wall with my room. Her door was always closed when she was in there. I knocked, timidly.

"I'm not going." Her voice was unwavering.

"It's me. Papá and Bernie left already."

"Please be so kind as to read the sign on the door."

A Do Not Enter sign hung in the middle of her white door. Below the yellow letters, Rosalinda had scribbled with a red marker: SPECIALLY LITTLE GEEKS. That was a reference to me, her geeky little brother. Spelling was not Rosalinda's strength.

"Are you decent?" I asked.

"No. I'm indecent."

"I need to ask you something. It's really important." There was silence on the other side. I knew that was as close to "Come in" as I was going to get. I turned the knob and opened the door slowly. She was lying horizontally on her bed reading. The novels Rosalinda read usually had shirtless men embracing women with glassy eyes and half-opened mouths, the sure look of some kind of intestinal pain. This book, however, had a familiar black cover.

"You're reading the Bible?" I said in shock. Seeing a Bible in Rosalinda's hands was as unlikely as seeing Papá dancing around the house in a tutu.

"Is that so astonishing?" She rested the open book on her stomach and looked at me, poised to defend herself. Rosalinda and I had constant battles over her reading choices.

"Is that for school?" I already knew the answer to my question, but I needed to warm Rosalinda up with some small talk.

"No, I'm reading Leviticus because I just love the way the guy writes. Of course it's for school."

"Leviticus?"

"Yup. Have you read it? What am I saying? Of course you've read it. You've read everything."

"I'm familiar with it," I said with as much nonchalance as I could muster. "What class?"

"World History." Rosalinda yawned. She'd had her best friend, Petra, for a sleepover, and I knew for a wakeful fact that they had stayed up talking until 3:16 a.m.

"Leave it to Mount Carmel to use the Bible for a history book." I tried to make her laugh, or at least smile, but all I got was another yawn. "By the way, what did you say to Papá to get off from going to church?"

"Cramps. What about you?"

"Bernie told him I had a sore throat."

"Great! You should give your sore throat a rest." She made a "go away" motion with her fingers. "I need to finish this before I have to start cooking Sunday dinner. Cramps aren't going to keep me from that." She lifted the book above her face. When I didn't move, she lowered it again. "Okay, what do you want?"

I sat gingerly on the edge of the bed. She eyed my movements the way a cat eyes an over-friendly dog.

"I have a family question." I hoped I didn't sound too anxious.

She flipped quickly to her side and propped her jaw on the palm of her hand. I guess even a question from your geeky brother is better than Leviticus. "Shoot," she said, pretending she could care less, but I detected interest. "But remember, you get what you pay for."

"Ha, ha!"

"Seriously, could you do my report? It would be a piece of cake for a genius like you. All you have to do is give four examples of how women were treated when Leviticus was written."

"You should ask Papá. He's the real Bible expert in the house. Besides, that's so easy, even *you* can do that," I replied. The foot attached to her long leg reached the small of my back. "Ouch!" I wanted to talk about what was eating me, but it was hard not to jab at her. She was such an easy target.

"Speak now or forever hold your peace," she commanded.

"Is that piece as in P-I-E-C-E?"

It took Rosalinda a few moments to spell the word in her head. "That's hilarious." She flashed me a fake grin.

What can I tell you? I'm a moron when I'm stressed. I cleared my throat. It was time to get serious. "It's about Bernie," I managed to say.

"What about him?" Her immediate and concerned response confirmed for me once and for all that Bernie was her favorite brother. Bernie was beyond reproach. She happened to be right, but it still hurt a little, the way she was always so ready to defend him.

"Why do you think that he never goes out with anyone? I

mean all your friends are always after him. Petra has orgasmic spasms whenever he even glances in her direction, which is not often. And she's supposed to be sizzling."

"Okay, okay. Hold on a second. Let's go through what you said step by step. Let's *ANAL*ize things, as you like to say. What do you know about 'orgasmic spasms'?"

"Everyone knows about orgasmic spasms. It's common knowledge."

She lifted her eyebrows. They were stuck up there for about ten seconds.

She sighed. "You're how old? Thirteen?"

"Fourteen next month."

"Fourteen going on forty!" She sighed.

"Okay, okay, you don't have to get a cow over it."

"It's 'have a cow,' not 'get a cow,' and you shouldn't be quoting Bart if you've never watched the show."

"Who's Bart?"

"I rest my case." She sat up and scooted to the head of the bed, where she propped a pillow behind her. "Why doesn't Bernie go out with anyone?" She scrounged her eyebrows in my direction. I could tell that she wasn't pondering the question. She was penetrating my skull, trying to decipher the gray hieroglyphics that twisted chaotically in there. "Now, why would you ask such a question?"

"I just find it strange. He's eighteen, extremely handsome,

has an after-school job at Papá's garage, so he has money, and I've never seen him go out with anybody."

"And that bothers you because . . ."

"I'm worried about him?"

She gave me her bull-detector grin. "Try again," she said.

I took a deep breath. "Do you think he might be—?"

"No," she cut me off. "He's not." Then she rubbed her chin à la Sherlock Holmes. "But it is very interesting that *you* should be asking me that."

I gush of hot blood rushed from the tip of my toes to the top of my head. I started to get up.

"Wait. Sit." She waited for me to obey. I sat on the bed reluctantly. "I'm going to answer your question."

"What question?" I asked.

"Why Bernie doesn't go out with girls."

Oh, that question.

"Bernie is a noble kind of guy."

"You mean as in he moves around a lot?"

"What?"

"Oh, *noble.* I thought you said *mobile.*"

"You are such an idiot." She paused to collect herself and then continued: "First of all, Bernie goes out with more girls then you know about. He just doesn't date girls from Mount Carmel. Why, you ask? Most girls at Mount Carmel are not like *moi.* Most of them are like Petra—you know: beautiful but traditional. What do you think would happen to Petra, for example, if Bernie asked her out?"

"They'd have to call the coroner?"

"Do you want a serious answer to your question or not?"

I nodded. The focus of the conversation had shifted from me to Bernie, so I was fine.

Rosalinda's face was suddenly serious. "The reason Bernie doesn't ask Petra out, or any one of countless girls at Mount Carmel, is because those kind of girls want a serious relationship and Bernie is waiting until the absolute right girl comes along. He doesn't like to date the same girl more than once or twice. If he dates a girl more than twice, that's probably the one he'll marry. Besides, he knows that if he went out with anyone from Mount Carmel, that poor girl would be a goner, heart-forever-broken, not the same again, ever." She waited a quick moment and then went on, "And even if that poor girl ever managed to eventually marry someone else, she would be doing so out of a sense of hopeless resignation. You follow?"

It took me a few moments to fully understand what she was saying, and then I nodded. Rosalinda for once in her life was right. All the girls at Mount Carmel were already half in love with Bernie. If he went out with them, they would want to bear him children right there on the spot. Shoot, if he was a sheik and they were only one of a thousand wives, they'd stand in line and take a number. "I follow," I said in agreement.

It was the right time, I thought, to take my inquiry one step further. "It's just that there are some things about him. . . ."

"Such as?"

"He cooks. He even bakes. He makes cupcakes with pink frosting."

Rosalinda laughed. "Oh, I get it. And real men don't do that, right?"

"Not according to Papá, they don't. Real Mexican men don't cook or bake."

"Yeah, right, if it were up to Papá, I'd have to do all the cooking and dishwashing and cleaning around here. Thank God there's at least one person that helps me." She shot me her deadliest killer glance. "By the way, who eats the cupcakes?"

"Not all of them," I answered guiltily. Then, I added, "And he's always going with you to the mall to help you shop."

"Well, sometimes I need a man's advice."

"Why? Because you want to impress Manny Luongo?" Manny Luongo was the quarterback at Mount Carmel and, next to my brother, the hottest guy at school. I had just the night before discovered that Rosalinda had a thing for him.

"How . . . ?" she said, eyes narrowing. "You were eavesdropping on me and Petra again, weren't you?"

"That's not all," I said, trying to change the subject. "Bernie drives a light-blue Prius!"

"So?" Rosalinda asked, mystified.

"Papá says it's a sissy's car."

"Oh, here we go again. Papá. Papá. Papá. Do you believe everything Papá says? You think I believe everything Papá says or the nuns at school tell me? I'm an independent woman, buddy. You should try that kind of thinking yourself instead of accepting everything that Papá says as gospel truth. Besides, who washes that baby-blue car about twenty times a week, which is almost as many times as he takes a shower?"

"I don't like to see him drive a dirty car. It doesn't reflect well on the family. And I take lots of showers because I like to smell clean."

"And you use my moisturizer because . . ."

Once again blood made its customary trip from toe to hair follicles. How did Rosalinda know? I was so careful. "It's good for pimples," I mumbled.

"And who reads *Vogue*?" She was looking straight at me.

"You do."

"And who else?"

"Only when I'm in the bathroom."

"Ewwww! No wonder you spend hours in there. Have you ever seen him even open that magazine?"

"Who?"

"Bernie. Who else are we talking about?"

She was annoyingly right yet again. I had never seen Bernie read *Vogue*. "Why does he buy it, then?" I asked, confused.

"He buys it for us, for you and me. Mostly he buys it for you. I told him once I preferred *Cosmo,* but he said, and I quote, 'Luis likes the fashions in *Vogue.*' Are you getting all this?"

I was stunned. I was a pretty smart guy. I never got a B in my life. I was also very perceptive. I could tell if Rosalinda was wearing a blouse from Abercrombie and Fitch or Anthropologie. But it never occurred to me, never, not for one microsecond, that Bernie bought *Vogue* for me to read, which I did every month, religiously, from cover to cover, and not just when I was in the bathroom.

I stopped. I blinked. Then I rubbed my right eye with my index finger. Rosalinda never cleaned her room, and dust was always flying everywhere. "Remember when Papá found the computer open to the website on baking recipes? He was so mad at Bernie. God hates a *maricón,* he said. Especially a Mexican one." My voice was low. I could hardly say the word. It had sounded nasty when Papá said it, but it sounded ten times worse hearing myself say it.

Rosalinda folded her legs and then crawled on her knees to where I was. Before I could do anything, she grabbed me by the shoulder and planted a big wet kiss on my cheek.

"Okay, okay," I said softly, pretending to pull away, "don't get a cow."

She sat on her haunches on top of the bed, not letting go of me. "And what did Bernie do when Papá said that?"

I couldn't speak. There was a lump in my throat the size

and texture of one of those Mexican limes that Bernie liked to squeeze on his chicken soup. "He told him not to say that kind of stuff ever again. That it was not something Jesus Christ would ever say. That it was a bunch of *mierda,* and that God — that God made all kinds of Mexican guys."

She moved closer to me and sat on the edge of the bed. "Have you ever, before that day, heard Bernie use that word?"

I shook my head.

"You know why he did that?"

I shook my head again.

"It was like he was defending someone, wasn't it?" She was almost whispering in my ear.

I nodded.

"He did it for you. He was defending you. You! Luis. Our geeky little Mexican guy, made just right by God."

The green lime that had been stuck in my throat exploded, and I was suddenly crying. I buried my head in Rosalinda's chest. I don't know how long we sat there next to each other. Finally, I wiped my eyes on my arm. Rosalinda lifted a corner of her chartreuse T-shirt to dry my cheeks. "Bright colors make you look fat," I said.

She smiled and rubbed the back of my head. "Told you I needed a guy's advice, didn't I? Now, get out of here. Go to the bathroom and read your magazine."

I stood up.

"But don't take forever," she warned.

I looked at her one more time and smiled. Then I slowly walked out.

I noticed, as I was walking to my room, that my steps were lighter, so much lighter.

Lexicon

NAOMI SHIHAB NYE

Hearts, like doors, will (open) with ease
to very, very little keys,
and don't forget that two of these
are "Thank you, sir," and "If you please."
　　　　　　　　— Traditional

1.
Certain words
got lost on their way —
why should they pull us
down their twisted paths?

Using them feeds them.
War is *raw*, backward and forward.

Terror contains *rot* and *tore*.
Well, of course.
It would not be filled
with *toast* or *lamp*.

Because my Arab father said,
I love you, habibi,
darling was everywhere.
Sweetness emanating from trees.
Mint in your tea?
Ahlan wa sahlan — you are all welcome.
Friends, strangers, came right in.
Sat in a circle, poured, and stirred.
Teacups steaming on an oval tray.

Being a good example —
why not?
(I was half-baked, mix of East and West,
balancing flavors.)
When they said, *May we tell you about Jesus?*
my father said, *He was my next-door neighbor!*

Because my father said, *Eye of my eye,*
heart of my heart, I felt surrounded —
soft love cocoon. He went outside to
smell the air. It spoke to him.

He crossed the creek,
took a turn.

How much you could own without owning.
Soft hope tucked into branches.
Down the block and up the hill.

My friend's dad said,
Let's get rolling, girls.
He was brusque, tough.
He drank beer and spat.
You're not leaving this house
till you finish your work.
My father's tongue had no *bitch*
hiding under it.

Mine said *friend* to everyone.
You don't even know her, Dad.
I'll know her sooner if I call her friend.

He was Facebook before it existed.
Only Arab on the block,
on the street, in the town,
he ran for president of the PTA.
Maybe not, said my mom.
But he won.

All his friends voted for him.
The Italians, the French Canadians.
If someone said, *I never met an Arab before!*
he would beam.
If someone spoke rudely,
he softened instead of hardening.
Oh, my, he'd say. *Let's start this
conversation again.*

Where have you gone, Daddy?
I need my personal Arab in a world of headlines.
I need your calm, loving voice like a rug on all the floors.

He hated chaos,
fighting,
wars.
He said, *Let's get more information.*
Man of gentle words,
could we bury nasty ones
in a graveyard now?

Then the earth would be polluted.

Tie them into sacks,
pitch them into lakes?
Then the lakes would be strange.

Words that never helped us?

Holding someone above.
Words aimed in anger.
Words that made walls.

Maybe we need a giant campfire,
all the dry twigs of sad words piled on top.
Light them carefully, say good-bye.
Fold your hands as they sizzle and fly, ash into air.
This will not be a fire to cook anything on.

2.
We need more words like
Comfortable
Bedrock
Pillow
Cake

Words that make us part of a whole.
Compass
Time
Chickadee
Shadow
Errand

Dreamboat
Canvas words.
Words with hems and pockets.
Umbrella, flashlight, milk.
Pencil, blizzard, song.
Words like parks to sit in.
Bench words. Did you ever notice how
pleasant and *pleasure* have *please* in them?
Except for that final *e*, which is waiting for
everybody to wrap their tongues around it.

In Geneva, Switzerland, I saw the longest bench
in the world. It stretched the length
of a block or two—
green with little snowdrifts
piled against the back—
no one sitting on it just then.
I wondered if my father ever sat on it.
Dreaming of words,
merci,
sesame,
I wanted to stay, sitting quietly,
soaking in memory,
till spring washed over
everyone, visible, invisible,

watching everyone pass,
in the neutral country,
the second United Nations city,
holding the thoughts.

Remembering my father's daily sweetness,
the way some people make you feel better
just by stepping into a room.
He loved the freshness of anything—
crisp cucumbers, the swell of a new day.
The way skin feels after being washed.
I'm happy to see you!
The day just got happier.

But dying, this lover of life said sadly,
My dilemma is large.
Nothing had become the world he dreamed of.
He wanted
simple times, people making room
for fun, for words.
Saying *darling* to fresh minutes lined up.
Shookrun—thank you—to legs strong enough to walk.
Shookrun to light coming over the fields.
Shookrun to light touching the houses.
Shookrun to everyone we haven't met yet.

Especially the nice ones.
Yes to all forgotten ones.

And then there would be language worth trading.
Words deserved by human beings, all deserving respect.
Coins and plums and an endless kiss
no one saw you get or give.

ABOUT THE EDITOR

MITALI PERKINS has spent most of her life crossing borders. She was born in India, but by the time she was eleven, she'd lived in Ghana, Cameroon, London, New York, and Mexico. Mitali's family settled in California just in time for middle school: she was the new kid again, in seventh grade, the year everybody barely makes it through.

"My biggest lifeline during those early years was story," Mitali says. "Books were my rock, my stability, my safe place, as I navigated the border between California suburbia and the Bengali culture of my traditional home."

She studied political science at Stanford and public policy at U.C. Berkeley, but turned to education — Mitali taught middle school, high school, and college — and fiction. Her protagonists are often strong characters trying to bridge different cultures or to promote justice. Mitali lives in the Bay Area with her husband, a pastor, and is a lecturer at Saint Mary's College of California.

ABOUT THE CONTRIBUTORS

CHERRY CHEVA (full name: Cherry Chevapravatdumrong) is originally from Ann Arbor, Michigan. She is the author of *She's So Money* and *DupliKate*. She is a writer and producer for *Family Guy* and lives in Los Angeles. "A lot of people watching the *Family Guy* credits think my name is fake," says Cherry. "It's not. It's just Thai."

VARIAN JOHNSON is the author of the Jackson Greene series, *The Parker Inheritance*, and other books for children and teens. He was born and raised in Florence, South Carolina, and attended the University of Oklahoma, where he received a BS in civil engineering. He also received an MFA in writing for children and young adults from the Vermont College of Fine Arts and lives in Austin, Texas. "I was the typical high-school geek," he says. "I played the baritone in the marching band, was a member of the Academic Challenge Team, and counted my Hewlett-Packard 48G calculator as one of my most prized possessions."

G. NERI, author of *When Paul Met Artie: The Story of Simon & Garfunkle; Hello, I'm Johnny Cash; Ghetto Cowboy;* and other books for young readers, is a storyteller, filmmaker, artist, and digital-media producer. He taught animation and storytelling to inner-city teens in Los Angeles with the groundbreaking group AnimAction, producing more than three hundred films. "I'm Creole, Filipino, and Mexican—or as I like to call it, Crefilican. On top of that, my daughter is also German. If America's the melting pot of the world, then we're perfect examples of how diverse this country really is." Although he lives on the Gulf Coast of Florida, he and his family spent a year in Berlin, where he was often able to corral extra subway seats.

NAOMI SHIHAB NYE was born in St. Louis, Missouri. Her father was a Palestinian refugee, her mother an American of German and Swiss descent. Naomi grew up in Jerusalem and San Antonio, Texas. She is considered one of the leading female poets of the American Southwest as well as a major voice in children's literature. She is the author of *Habibi*, an award-winning novel for children, and *The Turtle of Oman*. She received her BA from Trinity University in San Antonio and continues to live and work there. "Writing is the great friend that never moves away," says Naomi.

MITALI PERKINS, author of *You Bring the Distant Near*, which was long-listed for the National Book Award and named a Walter Honor Book, and other books for young readers, was born in India and immigrated to the States with her parents and two sisters when she was seven. Bengali-style, the three sisters' names rhyme: *Sonali* means "gold," *Rupali* means "silver," and *Mitali* means "friendly." "I had to live up to my name because we moved so much," Mitali says. "I've lived in India, Ghana, Cameroon, England, New York, Mexico, California, Bangladesh, and Thailand."

OLUGBEMISOLA RHUDAY-PERKOVICH is the author of *8th Grade Superzero* and *The Civil Rights Movement* and is the co-author, with Audrey Vernick, of *Two Naomis*, which was nominated for an NAACP Image Award. She is featured in several books on writing: *Real Revision, Seize the Story, Wild Ink,* and *Keep Calm and Query On;* is a contributor to the essay collection *Break These Rules;* and is a member of The Brown Bookshelf and We Need Diverse Books. She has a master's in educational technology with a concentration in English education. "I was the new kid at school many times over, in more than one country," says Olugbemisola. "I now live with my family in Brooklyn, where I write, make things, and need more sleep."

DEBBIE RIGAUD was born in Manhattan, but the Rigaud family packed up the kids and headed to East Orange, New Jersey. "My parents never fully transitioned to Jersey living," says Debbie. "My childhood was happily spent heading back to Brooklyn for doctors' visits, summer vacations, ripe plantains—every excuse in the book." She has written for many magazines, including *Entertainment Weekly, Seventeen, Vibe, Cosmo Girl!, Essence, Heart & Soul,* and *Trace* magazine in London. Debbie is also the author of *Perfect Shot,* a novel for teens, and lives in Atlanta with her husband and daughter.

FRANCISCO X. STORK was born in Monterrey, Mexico, to Ruth Arguelles, a single mother from a middle-class family, and now lives in Boston. He is the author of several critically acclaimed novels, including *The Memory of Light, Marcelo in the Real World, Disappeared,* and *The Last Summer of the Death Warriors.* "Part of me left Mexico when I was nine, and part of me is still there," says Francisco.

GENE LUEN YANG is a former National Ambassador for Young People's Literature. He is the author and illustrator of *American Born Chinese* and *Boxers & Saints,* and co-creator of *The Eternal Smile, Level Up,* and *The Shadow Hero.* He has also written for *Superman* and *Avatar: The Last Airbender.* He was born in the San Francisco Bay Area after his father emigrated from Taiwan and his mother from Hong Kong. "In fifth grade, my mother took me to our local bookstore, where she bought me my first Superman comic book," he says, explaining his lifelong love of the genre. Yang attended the University of California, Berkeley, majoring in computer science with a minor in creative writing, and received his master's in education from Cal State, Hayward, where he wrote his thesis on using comics in education. He teaches writing for children and young adults through Hamline University.

DAVID YOO lived in Seoul, South Korea, from age three to eight, during which time he learned how to curse fluently in Korean. From eight years old to now, he is a lifelong New Englander, and the author of *The Detention Club, Stop Me If You've Heard This One Before, Girls for Breakfast,* and, most recently, a collection of essays for adults, *The Choke Artist: Confessions of a Chronic Underachiever.* He teaches in the MFA program at Pine Manor College and at the Gotham Writers Workshop.